MW01672272

As Death Stared Back

As Death Stared Back

Ajinkya Bhasme

PAPER TOWNS
PUBLISHERS

PAPER TOWNS
PUBLISHERS

First published by
Papertowns Publishers
72, Vishwanath Dham Colony,
Niwaru Road, Jhotwara,
Jaipur, 302012

As Death Stared Back
Copyright © Ajinkya Bhasme, 2019

ISBN Print Book - 978-93-87131-36-1

All rights reserved. No part of this book may be reproduced or transmitted in any form or by any means, electronic or mechanical, including photocopying, recording, or by an information storage and retrieval system—except by a reviewer who may quote brief passages in a review to be printed in a magazine, newspaper, or on the Web—without permission in writing from the copyright owner.

Although the author and publisher have made every effort to ensure the accuracy and completeness of information contained in this book, we assume no responsibility for errors, inaccuracies, omissions, or any inconsistencies herein. Any slights on people, places, or organizations are unintentional.

Front cover image: Isabella Mariana, https://www.pexels.com/photo/woman-s-face-1988681/
Back cover image: Alf Marty, https://pixabay.com/photos/child-child-at-the-window-window-2667485/
Cover Typography: Somesh Yadav

For all the motherly figures I am fortunate to have.

For Vandana Bhasme, my biological mother,
who is my everything.

For Ankita Agrawal, my amma from my dance family
who knows me the best in the world.

For Kanchan Fulmali, my maoshi,
who is like my second mom.

For Heidi Scarpelli, my inspiring American mother
who always sends me positivity from a land far away.

And for all the mothers in this universe
who love their children beyond mere words can describe.

Sometimes reality is scarier than nightmares

What is the truth, but a perception of reality?
And when the reality is blurred,
Your eyes will bleed before you see the absolute truth.

Chapter 1

Sanjana lay in her bathtub with just her face above the dark tar-like water. Her brown hair created a web on the shiny surface of that thick liquid just above her pale face. She was not blinking. Her gaze was fixated at the white ceiling of her bathroom. Her big brown eyes were terrifyingly constant, lifeless, with dilated pupils looking at something.

The ceiling started to project blue and orange flames. Her head began submerging slowly in the ebony water that reflected the hellfire projections on the ceiling.

The web of her hair got heavier as the fire started to move across the ceiling to the walls. Her gaze, however, did not move even slightly as her head sank. Her hair lurched inside the sable bath as if it were pulled down. Yet she did not blink. She did not want to miss the sight of him after all.

The fire projection moved from the wall to the bathroom floor and soon engulfed the entire bathtub in a real infernal conflagration.

Her eyes and nose started to submerge in the raven fluid, but she managed to keep her eyes open. The water had begun to boil, creating bubbles at the surface as she submerged further in. But before the black lava swallowed her, he appeared on the ceiling exactly where her gaze was fixated.

There he was, in flesh, her deceased husband, who appeared for a fraction of a second before she sank completely below the dark surface.

The water had started to boil violently like a volcano ready to erupt. The fire grew as the flames started lightly brushing the ceiling. Grey smoke enveloped the entire bathroom. The water in the bathtub was evaporating and the level had begun to slowly descend.

Suddenly, her hands jumped out of the water, desperately clenching the rim of the tub. She used its support to barely get her face out and breathe.

As soon as she came up, she let out a terrified scream with her eyes back to normal. There was struggle beneath the turbulent murky surface as if she was struggling to get out. Her hands went back inside the water dreadfully searching for the stopper.

With her face sticking out, and legs vigorously moving beneath the surface, her eyes continuously moved across the room helplessly searching for something.

And there he stood, a young boy, about 5-years-old, in the middle of the flames, silently looking at her. She looked at him, slightly afraid, but the fire did no harm to him.

Her hands had found the stopper. She pulled it out. The water was being consumed in a dreaded whirlpool. As the level rapidly went down, so did the flames.

The boy watched as Sanjana's body draped in a white saree started to show itself. She had no hair on her head. The boy just stood there in his ash-laden, white funeral clothes as the water went down completely.

Sanjana was not alone. She was on top of another body that had held her from below. He had clutched her tightly by the waist. He was resting on something that looked like a pyre of sticks and straws. She couldn't move or get away from his lifeless grip.

She realised that her hair had been pulled apart and she was lying on the corpse of her dead husband going 'sati'. Her son slowly approached her and began to speak. His lips moved, but his voice was like his father's.

"Don't be scared, darling. You shouldn't be afraid of my voice," he said gently.

"Be afraid when you can't hear me," the corpse finished.

A scream from the other room woke her up. She got up in her bed and swiftly moved out like the nightmare had not affected her at all. She rushed to her son's bedroom.

"What's the matter, Manu?" she asked him, hugging a six-year-old Abhimanyu.

"I saw him again. But he was different," said Manu shivering with fear.

Sanjana realised that his pyjamas were wet.

"Let's get you changed, okay baby?"

Manu was embarrassed, but he nodded without eye contact.

"It's okay, baby. It happens to everyone." She gave him a fresh pair of clothes, "I promise, I won't look."

"Can you come with me to the bathroom at least? I am scared," said Manu.

"Well, of course, dear."

Sanjana escorted Manu to the bathroom and switched all the lights on, "Look there is nothing here. And it smells like lemons."

Manu peeped inside, half-hidden behind Sanjana. She looked at him and exactly knew what scared him and why.

"Don't worry, Leena aunty has cleaned it spotless today. And the smell of lemons shoos away the ghosts," she said gently smiling at Manu.

"I will keep the door open," said Manu.

Manu quickly did his business, changed and ran out. Sanjana went back inside to put his dirty clothes in the basket and flush.

"May I sleep next to you, mummy?" yelled Manu from his mother's bedroom.

"Sure, beta. I will be there in a minute," Sanjana said with her voice muffled in the sound of the flush.

She picked up his dirty clothes and put them in the laundry basket near the bathtub. She turned around to exit, but something caught her attention. She paused for a moment and turned right back.

And there it was again that night, near the drain, sticks, straws, and a bunch of hair.

Chapter 2

The clock had struck thirteen. Time was absconding as he began to slip into the abyss. There was nothing that she could do to bring him back. She had screamed her lungs out and now her abhorrence for time had made her coil like a snake.

He was not coming back, and she had to live with it for the rest of her life.

A man dressed in white came close to Sanjana and placed a hand on her shoulder.

"It's time to take the body away," he said in a broken whisper.

Sanjana did not hear. Her eyes were sore from crying for the last ten hours. She had spoken nothing either. After the last call she made to her mother speaking between heart-breaking sobs, she had gone completely silent.

She lay silently on the floor near the body, refusing to look at it or touch it. She just wanted to be close to it.

A group of four men, dressed in white funeral clothes, picked the body that was covered in a white sheet and adorned with marigold flowers. They lifted it from the ground onto their shoulders.

They escorted the body out of the house as other men followed them on the streets. Sanjana was scared to look up. She did not have the heart to see them take him away.

"I want to go to the crematorium too," Sanjana verbalised for the first time in hours.

"But ladies cannot go, beta," said her mother, "You have to be here in the house."

Sanjana did not respond. She got up from the floor, lifted her white saree, wore a pair of chappals and marched outside.

Her mother, Ratna, rushed after her to stop her, but her mother-in-law stopped Ratna from going after her.

"Let her go, she needs to find peace or she will never recover from this," said Arati barely even able to speak, trying to be strong.

"How are you managing to hold up so well?" wept Ratna, "I am unsure how to process this loss, and I can imagine it would be more difficult for you."

"I..." stuttered Arati, "I am not holding up. I can never... Life is not fair, but we all have to be there for Sanjana. She is frail."

Ratna hugged Arati as she collapsed in her arms. Arati began to wail in despair as Ratna wept too.

Ratna mustered some strength between her sobs as she looked up and prayed loudly, "If there is a God, I pray to her, never let a mother, ever, bear the sorrow of seeing her child die."

Arati yowled in Ratna's arms, not knowing what to do.

"Mom... Mom, wait for me!" yelled a five-year-old Abhimanyu running behind Sanjana.

Sanjana looked back. Abhimanyu was dressed in his white funeral clothes, sprinting behind her, barefoot. Sanjana looked at him with concern and yelled, "Manu, be careful."

She ran back towards him and picked him up. The road was covered with gravels and stones. Manu's feet were dirty, and some fine stones had stuck to them. With the end of her untouched saree, Sanjana wiped the dirt off his feet.

"Why did you follow me? You should not be here," sighed Sanjana.

Manu shrugged and breathlessly formed a sentence, "Where…is…daddy…going?"

Sanjana gulped dry air. She did not know how to answer that question. She, herself did not know what would happen to the soul after the body is cremated.

"Daddy is going to heaven," she lied.

"Are we going there too?"

She remained silent and chose not to answer that question. She carried him to the crematorium. It was an open space with many men surrounding the pyre. She stood up on an elevated platform under a shed, far away from the crematorium, but close enough so that she could see the rituals. Her eyes began flooding again. She placed Manu down and stood right in front of him.

The sun was sinking in the auburn sky that prismed the insignia bred by the cremation. The doors of heaven were opening as the pyre was set ablaze.

'Would it be hurting him?' she thought to herself.

Manu squeaked from behind her in fear. She looked back at him.

"Manu, look at me," she said, staring into his eyes and taking his hand in hers. It was icy cold. She blew on them and continued with a broken voice.

"Don't be afraid. I want you to keep looking at me, nowhere else. I might look away, but you need to look at me, look out for me. It will be dark soon, so I need you to be brave. Can you do that for me, baby?"

Manu's breath was shivering. Sanjana shifted Manu in front of her with his back facing the funeral. Manu held Sanjana's hand and kept looking at her as instructed by her. Sanjana felt the heat of the fire warm her body. The flames were dancing on the rhythm of her pounding heart full of anguish.

Everyone except the 4 shoulders had left the crematorium. The fire was intensifying; the men began to leave.

Sanjana carried Manu and told him to keep his eyes closed. Manu closed his eyes. She marched near the pyre without looking at the men. Sanjana kept walking toward the pyre, staring into the fire with tears drying up before they even escaped her eyes.

She felt a familiar touch on her shoulder. It was her father-

"It's done, Sanju. Let's go home."

"Let me be here as long as I want. I promise I will come home."

He looked at her one last time that night and left, not knowing that the next sunrise for her was not going to be the same.

She sat down, hauntingly close to the fire, Manu standing beside her. Both of them with their backs turned towards the malevolent blazes. The flames crackled in the absolute silence of the night. The flesh inside them was melting, the bones were cracking. The wrath of fire grew taller disappearing into the lifeless sky.

"Sanjana, let's go home."

There was a hand near her face. But she refused to take it or even look at it. Every voice that she heard was overpowered by the screeches of the fire.

Manu stood there in the monstrous shadow cast by his mother, not entirely certain what was happening. His eyes were on her. He wanted to console her, but he did not know how to. He knew that from that moment on, he had to be there for his mother no matter what. He had to be her one strong support in all walks of life.

Manu slept in his mother's lap, waiting for her to get up. She did not move a muscle and kept staring at the swaying shadows of the smoke. The fire was getting cold, its shrieks had started to sound like light whispers. She knew it was time to say goodbye.

The sun was still not up. She woke Manu and asked him to stand away from the moribund fire. There was one last thing she had to do.

She removed her *mangalsutra* and threw it into the pyre. The moment the surface of the *mangalsutra* touched the fire, the fire blew a miniature explosion of raging hot pieces of wood like a ghoul inside was awakened.

Manu got startled and ran towards Sanjana stepping over a small piece of burning wood that got stuck to his foot. Sanjana turned around and saw that Manu had fallen down and his clothes were all ashen. She swiftly went to Manu and removed the stuck piece with her saree. Thankfully Manu was not hurt at all, but his heart was pounding outside his chest with fear.

"I saw him! In the pyre," Manu screamed loudly.

Sanjana looked at him askance.

"Mom, I saw him," he yelled again, breathlessly.

Sanjana carried Manu and rushed to leave. The pyre swallowed her necklace whole and let out an ominous cry. The log of woods and straws shifted and fell down.

"Keep your eyes closed, Manu," said Sanjana running away.

Manu slightly opened his eyes behind her. The logs had fallen and something that seemed like a terribly burnt hand emerged out of the ashes clutching her *mangalsutra*.

Manu gasped as Sanjana heard her husband's voice from behind-

"Will you not wait for me?"

Chapter 3

Sanjana poured the thick crimson beetroot juice in a glass tumbler and carried it from the kitchen into the living room.

A fifteen-year-old Manu was sitting in his chair across a study table with his Algebra textbook open. His head was hanging in his hands, carrying the weight of a complicated math problem. Across him was a man bearing a dense moustache that outlined his crestfallen lips. His serious gaze was hidden behind his rectangular rimless glasses.

Manu kept looking at his empty notebook and began fidgeting with his pen, drumming the tabletop, believing that if he stared at the page hard enough, the answer might present itself to him.

"Here, Manu."

Sanjana kept the glass of juice in front of him. She wiped her damp hands on her *kurta* and snatched Manu's pen. She quickly wrote an equation on his empty notebook and gently smacked his head.

"Such a simple problem, Einstein!"

Sanjana grew up being constantly bullied by her unkind classmates. She had always been slightly overweight and dark. Despite being from one of the wealthiest families in the state, she was teased every single day for her appearance. Her early childhood resulted in her reclusive personality. She never wanted to be thin; she never even tried, 'why should I fit into their expectations?' she always asked herself. She befriended her books and became one of the most sought-after scientists in the country.

"Ma'am, you seem to be able to do this quite well yourself," declared the man forcing a smile, "Why do you even need me? Besides, I charge a lot."

"Sir," said Sanjana returning Manu his pen, "I have home-schooled Manu all these years myself. He is a very smart kid, but I cannot take any risks. It is his 10th boards this year and he wants to be the top ranker. My sources tell me that you are the best."

The man placed his spectacles on the table, looked at Manu, leaned towards him and verbalised, "I don't take many students per year, Manu. I will require your full dedication if I choose to teach you."

He leaned further in. Sanjana observed Manu's face from a distance. He looked at the teacher right into his eyes.

"So, tell me, Manu," said the teacher, "What do you dream of becoming?"

Sanjana's brow got together in a look of curiosity. Manu pierced his teacher's gaze and firmly stated,

"A dream is manufactured from a deep psychological place buried in our unconscience. It is the product of conflicts between our deepest, darkest desires and what others expect of us. Often, the dreams that come across as sweet to us are not really positive. They are the result of anguish, realising imagery that could be. Every dream, sir, is technically a nightmare. Like a wolf in sheepskin. Many cultures believe that dream catchers block nightmares and help to realise your sweet dreams. But what it really does is just make the wolf hungrier, projecting itself as an alibi while lurking to hunt an entire village. So, the answer is- no, No sir, I do not 'dream' of becoming anything. I will become an architect though."

Sanjana's pressed lips turned into a smile just around the corner as she looked at the teacher expecting a reply. There was silence for a moment.

"Well," said the man, "That was impressive. Although I don't completely agree with you. But I must say, for a boy of your age, pretty darn good."

Manu looked at Sanjana and smiled. He turned his book around to orient it right side up for the teacher.

"Are these the things that you don't agree about?"

Manu presented a list of words he had used that the teacher potentially did not agree to. The teacher read it keenly before speaking, "How-

How, did you know?"

Manu cocked his head, raised an eyebrow and said, "Your body language gave it away. It was pretty easy to read, actually. Every time I said something you did not like, your nostrils flared a little."

The man seemed very impressed. He nodded in agreement with a satisfactory smile. Sanjana looked at Manu with extreme pride; she had taught him well.

"Don't be cocky. Finish your juice," commanded Sanjana.

She escorted the teacher to the drawing-room and enquired, "So, Kartik sir, when would you like to start?"

"It's Dr Kartik," he corrected, "I can start from tomorrow. But let's discuss my fees first…"

"That will not be a problem, Dr Kartik," interrupted Sanjana while Dr Kartik moved through the hall looking at the family picture near the entrance. Manu looked like he was about two or three years old.

"I am the only daughter of the man who owns the Malhotra Empire. I earn pretty well myself. So, your fees should be no problem."

Dr Kartik sighed. He realised where Manu gets his slight arrogance from. He turned around to face Sanjana and nodded in agreement.

Sanjana accompanied him to the door. He opened the door and stood at the doorframe, facing her to ask one last question.

"Mrs Sanjana, I would like to meet Manu's father too," he pointed at the picture.

Sanjana paused for a moment looking at the picture, then sighed, "Punit passed away about 10 years ago. We don't like to speak about him."

"Oh, I am very sorry."

Before Sanjana could say anything, they heard a glass break from inside followed by a screech of a cat.

"Mom," yelled Manu from inside, "Poe spilled the juice and the glass broke."

Sanjana slapped her forehead and began whispering, "Breaking of glass is never a good sign. I will have to salt the house now."

Dr Kartik interrupted, "I am surprised. A brilliant lady like you believes in such superstitions."

Sanjana seemed distracted but she answered, "Don't worry, Dr Kartik, the house will teach you new things."

Sanjana saw that the wooden main gate of her house was open. The gate that blocked the view of the street from inside was naked.

"Did you leave the main gate open?" she asked, looking outside.

Dr Kartik quickly looked at the entrance and back at Sanjana and said, "I may have. I don't remember. Anyway, see you tomorrow. And I can't wait to meet Poe. I love cats."

Sanjana kept looking at the street, distracted. Her eyes did not meet Kartik as she said, "Poe doesn't like strangers. And, it is also a bad omen for people who hear a glass breaking. Be careful, doctor."

Kartik waved at her and walked through the front yard of her bungalow, absorbing the lavishness.

"And Dr Kartik," yelled Sanjana from behind and waved at him, "Never leave that gate open again."

Sanjana closed the door behind her.

The sun had already set but it was not dark yet. The street lights were already on ready to welcome darkness. Kartik shut the wooden gate on his way out, the security automatically locked it. He sat in his car, trying to forget the weird conversation. He turned the keys to bring the engine to life, but it refused to start. His sight got drawn at the street just around the corner. A man dressed in dark clothes walked towards the bungalow slowly on that crowded street. There was something not correct about it. As Dr Kartik saw his face in the streetlight next to the bungalow, his fingers froze, and his body was covered in cold sweat. The man in the picture entered her bungalow. Her dead husband.

The man punched in the numbers on the security keypad to the left of the sixteen feet tall wooden gate. After he punched the correct code, he rolled the gate to the right to open it.

Dr Kartik dialled Sanjana's number on his phone. Not reachable.

The man entered the main gate, turned around, and waved at Kartik and the next thing Dr Kartik heard was the main door creak shut.

Chapter 4

The water had disappeared from the tub. The fire was gone, and so were Manu and the corpse of her husband. Sanjana got out of the tub, soaking wet. She fumbled her way to the bathroom door, drenched. Her white saree looked pure and untouched like the black water had no effect on its colour. She took shaky steps towards the door, trying not to slip on the floor. Water from her saree was dripping everywhere. Her loose hair poured rivulets of the black liquid she had almost drowned in. She stood on the bathroom mat and squeezed her hair so that they stopped dripping.

She was shivering in her wet saree, ready to leave the bathroom when she heard a dragging sound from the room above. She knew Manu's bedroom was exactly above where she stood. She tried to ignore the sound, but she heard it again. It was like his bead was being dragged slowly and steadily.

From the judgment of where the voice could be coming from, she knew, it was right above where she saw her husband pinned to the ceiling. She desperately wanted to look, but she was too afraid. Her eyes were fixed at the bathroom door. She was still shivering on the doormat. Her pupils shifted to the right. From the corner of her eyes, she tried to look at the ceiling. Her body shook badly as her teeth began to clatter. Her pupils met the extreme right of her eyes and she realised Punit was still right there, fastened to the ceiling, looking at her. Or at least she thought he was.

Her body refused to move. Her pupils slowly moved back to look at the doorknob. She pursed her lips to exhale slowly. There was a whimper in her uneven breath as the sound of the furniture above her kept getting louder. Her pupils shot to the corner again. Punit was still looking at her, but he was also slowly dissolving in the ceiling above him. As he dissolved further in, the sound spawned from Manu's room amplified.

Sanjana's knees had begun to shiver as well. Punit had completely dissolved into the ceiling and the sound from Manu's room suddenly stopped.

Sanjana held her breath momentarily to comprehend what was happening. She turned around and looked up. There was nothing there. She exhaled swiftly and slowly tried not to make any noise. As her cold breath escaped into the empty bathroom, she heard a loud thud right above her followed by a terrifying scream for help from Manu.

Manu's terrified scream had her blood pumping. She instantly moved to the door and unlocked it. She got out of the bathroom and began climbing the polished wooden stairs leaving behind a trail of transparent water as she ran in the direction of Manu's room. She took every step carefully to avoid slipping and falling. The prints of her wet feet lay orphaned between the miniature puddles of water. She made her way to Manu's bedroom in minutes.

She opened the door to his bedroom. Her blood froze in horror as she saw, in the candescent light, the entire furniture in the room was upside down. The cabinets, the table, the chair, the lamp, everything was suspended by the ceiling. Manu's bed was the last. Sanjana saw his bed slowly creeping up the wall, to the roof, to stop right in the middle of the ceiling morbidly close to the fan. The five-year-old was in it.

An invisible force had held Manu upside down, facing the floor. He was screaming but his mouth was shut. His limbs were flailing dangerously close to the fan. Sanjana rushed inside with an intention to help Manu, but she did not know how to help him. Her wet saree had stuck to her body, weighing more than Sanjana could remember.

She jumped up a few times but soon realised it was meaningless.

"Manu," she yelled, "Baby, don't move, at all. I am getting a ladder from the kitchen. Do not move."

Manu stopped moving.

Sanjana quickly ran to the kitchen cabinet downstairs, still wet. She grabbed a small ladder and ran back up, as quickly and carefully as she could. Every step of the stairs was now wet, waiting for her to slip and fall. But the mother in her knew what risks to take.

She entered the room with the ladder in her hands. But before she could set it up, the ceiling sucked the ladder towards it like a powerful magnet. The ladder got horizontally pulled right into the light. The only source of brightness in that room exploded, leaving behind a room blanketed by darkness. The only dim light that made the room barely visible was from the passage.

Sanjana did not know what to do. She saw Manu float in mid-air, descending downwards slowly, chest first; behind Manu, she saw the cat-like eyes that glowed in that darkness. As Manu stood near the light that came from the doorway, Sanjana saw Punit's hands around Manu wearing their engagement ring, slowly loosening his grip.

Manu gasped and quickly ran into the arms of a teary Sanjana. She looked at Punit disappear into the darkness. She quickly carried Manu out and shut the door behind her. She realised Manu's heartbeat had increased drastically. She blew air in his ears and rubbed his cold hands.

As she moved away from the door, they heard a deafening bang from inside the room followed by lingering silence. Manu's eyes were already bloodshot. He closed his eyes with his hands as Sanjana slowly approached to see the contents of the room.

She opened the door slowly to a bright room with all the furniture as it was. Everything was intact, including the light as if nothing had happened. And just the ladder lay horizontally parallel to Manu's bed.

Sanjana quickly shut the door and looked at little Manu with his hands tightly wrapped around his eyes.

She bent down to pick him, but before she could, a draft of air chilled her bones and she heard a chuckle behind her ear.

Sanjana woke up to a disturbingly loud noise in the middle of the night. She knew something was not right. The nightmare had not affected her. Her eyes shot at the wall, it was 2am. She ran out of her room in the passage to find Manu fallen near the stairs, holding his ankle.

Sanjana went to him and cocked her head.

"You...you've grown," she said.

"Of course, mom," said Manu with pain, "No need to make fun of me. I know I am seven and should walk properly. I was just thirsty and going to the kitchen to grab water."

Sanjana kept looking at him strangely.

"What?" he asked.

Sanjana smiled and nodded her head to say 'nothing'.

"How did you manage to fall then?" she asked.

But before Manu could answer, she noticed a trail of water that started from his room and went up till the kitchen.

Chapter 5

It was still very early. The sun was yet to float above the surface of the horizon. The firmament was drenched in shades of orange and red.

Sanjana pressed the security key to the main gate and entered in. She was still carrying Manu in his dirty white clothes. She thought he had slept, but his tiny heart gave it away. The abnormal rhythm of his heart told her that he was still afraid.

Punit was a perfect husband but he was not a great father. Sanjana loved him eternally, which would perhaps be the reason why she heard him, she thought. Manu was a pre-mature baby who demanded extra care. His lungs were too weak to play in a stretch like other children. Punit had high expectations from Manu, in terms of sports and physical activities, but Manu always fell short. His regular visits to the doctor irritated Punit to an extent where he started getting negligent towards his health. Manu was smart even as a kid, even then, he could read the disappointment on his father's face. Their relationship had love, lots of it, but it was devoid of commitment, it was hungry with expectations, it craved for reciprocation. Sanjana took Manu's health as her primary responsibility which demanded a compromise in her work. Punit somehow always thought that things were better when Manu was not around. He never said it, but, to Manu, his body language gave it away.

Sanjana kept rubbing Manu's cold feet as she stood in front of the door. Manu's fear-induced hiccups were dying down finally. Sanjana bent down and retrieved a key from a flowerpot beside the door. She entered the empty house filled with her relatives. Everyone seemed to have been asleep. Sanjana shut the door behind her and kept rubbing Manu's feet as she carried him inside.

She placed him down in front of the bathroom. She went in, switched the water heater on and came out. She bent down to face Manu who was blowing warm air in his hands. He was shivering.

"Manu," she asked, "Why are you scared, darling?"

The time lag between his hiccups had reduced but they were not completely gone.

"It is just your imagination, beta. Don't think about it," she continued. She went to the kitchen, grabbed her phone from the table, fetched a glass of water and went back to Manu. Manu held his breath, drank the water and his hiccups were miraculously gone. Sanjana gave Manu her phone with his favourite puzzle game on.

"I am not able to solve this level," she said, "Can you help me?"

Manu quickly snatched the phone and got distracted. Sanjana's plan worked. She went back to the kitchen, put the glass down and looked around. The empty house was eating her up. Every single item the house contained had Punit's memories. She placed a hand on her mouth and began crying, cautious enough that Manu did not hear her.

She went back, gave Manu a warm bath, wrapped him in a towel, all fresh and dry, and carried him upstairs to his room. She changed him into a fresh pair of clothes and realised that Manu was sleepy. Sanjana's eyes were sore too, after the long night, they both needed to rest. She put Manu to bed, kissed him on the forehead and slowly stepped out of his room, wiping her tears.

As she closed the door, her mother stood there looking at her with despondent eyes. Sanjana ran across the passage and collapsed in her mother's arms crying loudly.

"Why...why...why?" she broke, "I can't believe he is gone. How will I manage without him?"

Her mother gently rubbed her back to comfort her. She was withholding from crying herself.

"You are a strong woman," she whispered, "You can figure it out. I know."

Sanjana calmed herself, loosening her grip. Ratna wiped her tears with her saree and tucked her hair behind her ears. Sanjana's gaze got caught by Arati, her mother-in-law, sitting alone at the bottom of the staircase. Sanjana descended the flight of stairs and sat beside Arati. She took her hand in hers and sat there silently with her, staring into nothingness with tired eyes. She dropped her head on Arati's shoulders.

"You have to be strong," said Arati in a broken voice. The house smelled of marigold flowers and death. Everyone was awake. The men were outside the house, talking loudly among each other.

"You have to be strong for the both of you now," continued Arati.

The door opened and Sanaja's father and father-in-law entered. They marched towards her.

"Beta," said her father-in-law, "We are going to the crematorium to collect the ashes and do the remaining rituals. Do you want to come?"

Sanjana refused. Tears were involuntarily flowing. She said, "I don't think I have the strength to face any more rituals. I bid my farewell already in the morning. Please..."

They both nodded at her and left.

Punit was the only son to his parents, so the house did not have any more family members to grieve.

Sanjana heard the door shut. But the doorbell rang again in no time. She opened the door. It was the neighbours. Sanjana felt a hand on her shoulders from behind. It was her mother.

"You go and rest," she said, "Arati and I will attend the neighbours."

Sanjana went upstairs and instead of going to her room, she headed to Manu's room. Manu was fast asleep in his bed. Sanjana lay beside him and closed her eyes.

She got distracted by the creak of the door. It was her mother, carrying a plate full of food. She carefully tiptoed across the bed and placed the food on the bedside table. She ran her hand through Sanjana's hair and gently whispered-

"Eat something, baby, it's already late. Finish your lunch and come down."

Sanjana nodded silently and Ratna left.

Sanjana caressed Manu's elbow to wake him up, but she immediately realised that he had spiked a fever. Manu slowly sat up in the bed, feeling weak. His mother carefully touched his forehead to confirm her prior judgement about his fever. His body was blazing. She quickly fed him a few morsels from the plate her mother had left. 'Maybe because of exhaustion and fear,' she thought. She put him back to bed and tucked him in a thick blanket that time.

After finishing the food on her plate, she carried the empty plate to the kitchen, leaving Manu to rest in his room.

"I was just coming upstairs to meet you," gasped Arati.

Sanjana looked around; everyone was outside. Her eyes met Arati again, with a hint of hope in them.

"All the rituals are done, beta," she continued, "The men are outside."

She gently held Sanjana's elbow and invited her to the door where her parents were waiting.

"Sanju, we are being dropped off now," vocalised her father, "Everything is done. And don't you dare feel alone, okay? We all are right here for you... for both of you. We may be old, but not weary. We stay just an hour away."

Sanjana hugged everyone. Her mother cupped her beautiful face, still sobbing, and brought her forehead to her lips.

"Please call. Promise me... promise me you will call if you need anything."

Sanjana nodded and bid them farewell. She saw them exit the main gate and close it on their way out.

She went back inside and began cleaning up. She did not want to wait for the maid to come next morning to tidy up the house. Besides, she needed a distraction, a goal that would keep her busy until she got tired and naturally fell asleep.

The sun was drowning on her life yet again, the day was coming to an end, and she knew she had to face the world all by herself from that day on. The evening songs of the birds seemed obstreperous to her, the voice of crickets was like nails on a chalkboard, and the silence of the moon was agonisingly loud.

She went upstairs to check on Manu. His fever had gone down, but he was very cold again. Manu was still in shock and his body had not recovered from the crematorium scare. She gave him her phone with the puzzle game on.

"I am going to bathe when I am back, we will play together."

Sanjana left him with the phone and marched into the bathroom downstairs. After the hard day, the hot water felt like it was washing away her sorrows. She was trying to figure out how to manage the house without Punit. She already worked but, she had to manage Manu and his education all by herself. She knew that Punit had no insurance policies in his name. Her brain couldn't think straight. Flashes of Manu's face sleeping on her lap in the crematorium kept appearing in her thoughts. They were all a big scramble of worries, whispering simultaneously in her ears. In those chaotic whispers, she heard the front door creak open and shut. 'Where is Manu going?'

she thought. She quickly closed the shower valve and half-dried herself with a towel. She haphazardly put some clothes on and went out of the bathroom.

She bumped into Manu who had a terrible fit of hiccups with her phone in his hand. Before she could say anything, Manu's terrified lips started to move,

"Dad's upstairs..."

Sanjana's body got instantly hit by a drop in gravity. She did not know what to feel. Part of her was happy and a part of her did not believe Manu. She collected her thoughts before speaking, but Manu interrupted her speaking between hiccups,

"He... he had a hammer... He... was... hurting me. He is..."

Sanjana opened her mouth to console him and tell him that it was not true, but her jaw got bolted shut when she heard the thunderous pounding of a hammer from her son's room. Her body was covered in goosebumps. The thuds had a peculiar wrath in them. She heard Punit yell Manu's name in angry grunts. What followed was footsteps outside the room. They were heading towards them.

Sanjana grabbed Manu, kept her phone on the kitchen table, and hid in the ladder cabinet with him. The cabinet was small, so she had to squeeze herself inside, but it was a haven for them. The only worry was that the door did not shut completely leaving a half centimetre gap.

The footsteps got louder as they finally halted across the kitchen table. She could not see him, but she could hear his grunts. He had stopped near the phone. Everything suddenly went silent. She tried to peek when suddenly, a loud bang startled her. Maun gasped, but she put her hand against his mouth to muffle his gasp.

Punit was hammering the kitchen table and began throwing all plates and utensils on the floor. Everything went silent again. But one thing that changed was, Sanjana could now see, she could see a terribly burnt hand holding something. She could swear it was Punit's hand.

He threw the content of his closed fist on the floor and marched away to the door. It slid across the floor to stop right in front of the ladder cabinet.

It was her *mangalsutra*.

And she heard the door creak open and shut again.

Chapter 6

Manu went to his bedroom to clean up the collateral damage to his clothes that Poe had done in the process of breaking the glass. Poe silently sat in a clean corner right next in the living room as if she owned everything, showing not even the slightest sign of guilt or remorse.

Sanjana was collecting the broken pieces of glass very carefully, one by one, trying not to get cut. As she threw the pieces into the bin, they clinked against the surface of the bin. She knew after she was done picking up the visible pieces, she would have to sweep and mop the floor. She got immersed in the rhythm. Like a monotone, the glass pieces provided her with a background track, and Sanjana began humming. But something soon went off-beat; the monotone missed a beat. She was confident that a beat had suddenly disappeared. She looked into the dustbin and saw a crumpled piece of paper in it. There was something strangely obscure about the paper. It seemed new, yet the corner that was visible to Sanjana showed a fresh elongated letter t in blue ink. The same fashioned letter the way Punit wrote when he signed. She picked up the paper ready to straighten it, to make it's content legible.

Poe suddenly hissed loudly. Sanjana got distracted and saw her staring at the door. Poe slowly walked to the door, back completely arched in attack. Every hair on her coat stood alarmed as her slow gait towards the door began. She paused at the door looking right at it; her back was completely arched and one paw was in the air. She seemed ready to attack. Poe was a tough feline even around familiar people, but Sanjana had never seen her exhibit such behaviour. Poe's hisses turned into a steady pacing monstrous growl.

Sanjana stood up scared, the piece of paper still in her hands. She was facing the door directly. She saw the doorknob move slowly. In the process of teaching Psychology to Manu, she knew her body had already triggered a response to the situation. In the classic response of fight or flight, she taught Manu a third and more common response in the modern time- freeze. Her muscles tightened as the doorknob turned completely. She kept staring in disbelief as the door swung open.

"Hi, Sanju," declared Punit, "I am home."

Poe hissed at him and pounced at him, scratching his knee through his trousers. With one swift kick of his leg, he shook Poe off. She kept walking towards him in low growls.

Punit took off his shoes at the door, placed them in the shoe rack next to it, and walked towards Sanjana in his socks. Sanjana was still immovable. Punit marched towards her, in flesh; he touched her, for the first time in a decade, and gave her a peck on the cheek. A sudden warmth filled her body. Her eyes had welled up.

He crossed her, stepping on the fine glass.

"Damn it," he exclaimed, "What the hell happened here?"

Sanjana said nothing.

Without waiting for her to respond, he marched straight upstairs. At the end of the staircase, he took a sharp left to head in the direction of his old bedroom. He went straight inside the bedroom and slammed the door behind him.

"Mom, is that you?" yelled Manu from upstairs coming in Sanjana's line of visibility. He went straight towards her bedroom following the voice.

"Come here, now!" commanded Sanjana in a loud whisper.

Manu came down quickly. Sanjana warned him from stepping on the glass and took him in front of the bathroom.

"What's happening, mom?"

"I just... I think... I just saw your father."

"What? You, I mean, did YOU actually see him?"

Sanjana nodded, holding Manu's hands. She was cold and so was he.

"I want you to get inside," she commanded Manu, pointing towards the bathroom, "And lock it. Do not come out till you hear me distinctly say so. Do you understand?"

"But mom," interrupted Manu, "Did you see him..." he emphasised on the word 'see', "...and not hear him like all these years..."

"Yes!" snapped Sanjana, "Now get in and do not come out."

Sanjana's bedroom door creaked. She shoved Manu in and closed the door. The last few inches of the door being closed gave Manu a decent peek at the glowing face of his father. He was back!

Punit marched down in his sweatpants and t-shirt. Sanjana moved away from the bathroom into the kitchen to avoid any suspicion. She watched Punit sit on the couch and turn on the TV browsing channels.

She took her phone and clicked a picture of Punit's side profile without him noticing. She quickly opened her chats and browsed for the contact saved as the 'Psychiatrist'. She texted him that picture and waited patiently for him to respond. She carried her phone with her and dawdled towards him.

Her phone chimed. She unlocked her phone to check her message.

'Who is this young man?'

'This is Punit, my husband.' She texted back.

Punit had stopped browsing the channels and had stopped on something peculiar. A decade ago, that movie used to be his favourite till he over-watched it and became nauseous of it. And that very moment, he seemed to be enjoying the movie.

Sanjana went and stood near the couch and cleared her throat loudly.

"Sanju," chuckled Punit, "You remember this scene?"

"Who... are... you?" Sanjana mumbled.

"Excuse me?"

"I said," loudly that time, "Who are you?"

"I am your husband," said Punit, with an innocent face, "And you may want to mind that tone."

Sanjana paced around the couch and stood between the television screen and Punit and growled in anger.

"You march into my house, unannounced, acting all innocent, claiming to be my husband, who, God knows how long ago, left me. You sit here, in his clothes, talking like him, behaving like him, watching his favourite movie. So, I will ask you again, nicely this time. Who the fuck are you?"

Punit stood up, enraged, his lips sucked into his teeth.

"I am your bloody husband," he screamed.

Sanjana's phone came to life. It rang like a knell in the room with a loud television in the background.

"Who is calling you at this hour?" questioned Punit looking at the time.

Sanjana looked at her phone- Psychiatrist calling...

She cancelled the call and continued staring into Punit's eyes.

"Prove it," she said.

"What?"

"Prove it to me that you are Punit."

"Are you out of your mind?"

"Prove it or get the hell out of my house!" screamed Sanjana.

Punit looked at her in anger. He took off his shirt and showed her the big scar on his back.

Sanjana was taken aback. The scar was exactly shaped like Punit's. He got the scar in his teenage in a biking accident. He put his t-shirt back on and sat down.

Sanjana fumbled back in disbelief and went straight to the kitchen. Her back facing the Punit that she had thought was long gone. Her phone sprang to life again, she answered it that time.

"Hello, Dr Shukla," she said, her attention diverted by the piece of crumpled paper on the table.

"Hello, Sanjana," spoke the calling end, "What's happening?"

"D-D- Doctor," stuttered Sanjana as she opened the paper.

On the paper were Punit's signatures, about twenty times. Each one looking more and more precise, but Sanjana was distracted by something else.

"Hello...can you please tell me you are okay?"

Sanjana's feet went cold as she saw the dead center of the page. In Punit's handwriting was Manu's name written, circled, and crossed out.

"And honey..." she heard a whisper from behind her as Punit leaned into her and continued, "The house is in my name, so I will not leave."

Chapter 7

The lights started to flicker. Manu was in her embrace, drenched in sweat, his heart thumping like gigantic tides crashing against rocks. She looked at his meek face. She was shaking like a leaf herself.

"Manu...Manu, look at me," she said, "It is okay. We are just dreaming."

Manu looked at her. But there was something wrong with his face.

The lights continued to flicker as a gush of cold wind came from the window behind Sanjana and screamed in her ears. In flashes of light and darkness, Manu's face changed slightly every time. It was like he was melting. His eyes and mouth were falling.

She held him tightly as the wind started making static sounds around her ear. In that dark prayer of the wind, she distinctly heard the key of a clock turning. It turned and turned as Manu melted into her arms, disappearing completely into nothingness. The lights went off, leaving behind a mansion of darkness.

The door to Sanjana's bedroom creaked open slowly revealing a small lantern on her bedside table. The floor had turned completely cold and a thick fog surrounded the whole passage. The key was still turning near her ear as she felt cold hands creep up her waist and grab her.

Her pupils dilated and the pearls of perspiration formed near her ears. She was immovable. Her paralyzed body couldn't resist the lifeless, icy hands that had a tight grip around her waist now. Her feet got lifted a few inches off the floor; she was levitating. She felt a warm breath down her neck and the hair there stood right up. Her jaw was glued shut; she could not scream or speak. All she could do was listen; he spoke,

"Darling, stop looking, start listening. Hear the darkness speak."

A chill travelled from her neck to her arms. She looked inside her bedroom to the only flickering flame of the lantern. Her heightened sense of hearing told her that the room was not empty. With the wind and the turning of the key, there was another monster present in that room. She heard a distinct low growl, and her eyes immediately adjusted.

Right next to the luminosity of the lantern were sharp teeth of a canine, its jaw gaping, with saliva dripping out of it. Its low growl was starting to get louder as Sanjana immediately realised, her levitating self was slowly being pushed towards the wolf. The key had stopped turning and the music box was devilishly unwinding. Punit's voice echoed in her ears as he whispered chants to her.

"Thank you, God, for the food today. Bless us and bless this food..."

He dropped Sanjana right inside the door, slammed it shut, and disappeared into the darkness.

The moment she touched the floor, a surge of lifelessness ran into her. She tried to open the door, but it was jammed. She turned around and faced the growling wolf surrounded by the bewildering fog. The animal growled ferociously and began circling her.

Sanjana stood still, trying not to move or breathe too heavily.

The animal walked past her and went towards her bed, disappearing back into darkness.

The faint notes of the music box were still monstrously playing, but the growling had disappeared. There was a new addition to the room. This was the first time she had heard a female voice. It came from the bed-she was humming a sad lullaby and wailing between notes.

Sanjana grabbed the lantern and lifted it up to shine the dim light on the bed. In the penumbra of the lantern, sat a woman in her bed, her back towards Sanjana, rocking her knee to put someone to sleep.

Sanjana turned around and ran towards the door. It was still jammed. She tried a few times, but her attempts were futile. She turned back around. The woman was now facing her, her hair dropping in front of her face. She had Manu's favourite stuffed toy in her laps. She was rocking the toy and singing the lullaby for it.

"Who are you?" asked Sanjana.

The woman did not respond. She started crying between her lullabies.

"Who are you?" Sanjana asked again.

The woman spontaneously busted in a fit of rage and shredded Manu's favourite toy with her bare hands, obliterating the soft toy violently while crying loudly.

"Stop it..." Sanjana screamed, "Stop. Who are you? Stop, please."

The music box suddenly stopped, but the growl had started again. The wolf was in the close vicinity. The darkness had acted her monologue, but her final act was still remaining. The door creaked open behind her and she heard Punit's voice again amidst the monstrous growl.

"Come on, Sanju, you know her."

And he blew the lantern into a pitch-black room and the wolf attacked her.

Sanjana shifted uncomfortably in her sleep, all muscles taut. The clock ticked showing 3:00am. Sanjana's closed eyes moved vigorously. She was still in her nightmare when suddenly her eyes opened wide.

It was the voice assistant in her room, which also acted as a Bluetooth speaker. She had her back towards it and it suddenly came to life.

"Now connected to Punit," it announced.

Sanjana's eyes slowly moved to the ceiling. She could see a shadow right on the ceiling in the light generated by the voice assistant. It appeared as if the shadow was sitting on the bed, right next to her. As the shadow moved slightly, her bed shifted.

Sanjana's blood ran cold. She slowly got up without looking at that side of the bed. She put on her house slippers and without turning back, headed straight into Manu's room.

She got inside his room to find him wide awake sitting in his bed.

"I heard that too," he said.

"Did you unlock your dad's phone?" Sanjana asked.

"Mom, I am smart, but I am still 9. We tried opening his phone before, but it is pattern protected. I don't know how to unlock it. Did you switch the phone on?"

"Yes," she lied.

Manu dropped on his back, feeling relaxed, and said, "Goodnight, mom. Shut the door when you leave."

Sanjana went in and kissed him goodnight and turned around to leave.

"Oh my God, what is that?" squealed Manu, pointing at her neck, "Mom, you are bleeding. And that wound...it...it... looks like a claw."

Chapter 8

"So, tell me about your dreams again," said Dr Shukla. Sanjana lay on the couch in his office, looking at the ceiling. The thick cyan walls ornamented with his degrees created a comfortable space for her to let out her feelings. His innumerable certificates in medicine, clinical psychology and about 30 years of experience helped Sanjana take a leap of faith.

"They started about a year after Punit died... they were comforting at first. But then, they started getting more and more intense, every dream much worse than the other. I used to get terrified of the dreams at first, but lately, the frequency of them has increased so much that it doesn't affect me in any way at all. But Manu, he still gets terrified..."

"How old is Manu now?" interrupted Dr Shukla.

"He will turn eight next month."

The psychiatrist was vigorously scribbling in his diary as he continued, "And how old was Manu when it all started?"

"He was six. And you know, doc? The first time I had a nightmare, I was sleeping right next to Manu, and coincidentally, we woke up at the same moment, gasping for air, like we both were being choked in our dreams. It happened a few times until Manu was seven and understood better how to explain his nightmares to me. That was the time when things got so bizarre to me that I no longer knew what to do. You see, Manu and I share some of these nightmares, to the exact detail, like our subconscience is somehow strongly connected. Right from the places where Punit appears in the dream, to the words he uses, everything we both see is absolutely the same. Sometimes it feels so real that it scares the life out of us."

"Why are you afraid?" inquired Dr Shukla, "Does Punit try to hurt you?"

"Not me..." said Sanjana looking at Dr Shukla writing, "... Manu. He is always trying to show me something or hold me or protect me."

"Protect you from what?"

"I am not sure, but there is this thing about the darkness. It seems like it speaks, it tells a story, and the story is not a pretty one. But somehow, in these long nightmares, Manu eventually is hurt or gets hurt. If it is neither, there exists an unsettling eeriness about the whole situation, which leads me to the premonition that something very bad is going to happen to him."

"But why, Manu? How was his relationship with his father when he was alive?"

"Not good, doctor, but not sour either. Manu, you see, is a physically weak child, so his father's expectations of sports and playing in the sun were not exactly logical. Manu became my first priority and Punit was never okay with that."

She explained how Manu was prematurely born and needed proper attention to stay in good health. She narrated the neglect as precisely as she could. Dr Shukla's pencil kept making scribbling noises between Sanjana's words. The pages of his diary were swiftly turning.

"Tell me about the voices," he said.

"Well," spat Sanjana, "It started the same time as the dreams. I have never really seen him in real life, only in my dreams, and very rarely in them either. It is always a silhouette or a limb or an object that he possessed. Even in my dreams, he would appear for a fraction of a second at times. It is always the voices. His voice is constantly present, like a song running on loop, just cold and lifeless."

Dr Shukla's phone vibrated on his table. He picked it up, swiped up and placed it back on the wooden table with it's facing down.

"Sit up, please, Miss Sanjana," he requested, "Our session has come to an end for the day. Here are some pills that I am prescribing."

He showed her the list containing a few medicines prescribed for daily usage.

"This is for you to sleep better and the other one will help you with your nightmares."

"What's wrong with me? Am I crazy?"

"We don't use that term here," he verbalised sternly, "Miss Sanjana, from my expertise, this seems like a manifestation of your mind for dealing with a big loss. Let me explain..."

He drew two circles on a blank piece of paper that he retrieved from his drawer.

"This small circle is your brain, and this big circle is your environment. You see, dreams are a result of how the brain perceives the environment in natural laws of restriction. The brain wants to be free, but it feels restricted, given the real-life limitations. It fulfils its deepest darkest desires in your dreams, the only place where you can tap into the deepest level of your conscience."

"So, you mean to say," interrupted Sanjana slightly offended, "That my conscience wants to hurt Manu?"

"Please, listen," says Dr Shukla in his heavy voice, "Your brain, Miss, is trying to deal with the loss of your husband by creating his image forcibly. Everything in your house certainly reminds you of him. Manu is simply facing the after-effects in those dreams. Given his situation with his father, your brain will paint as true a picture of the deceased- Punit as it can. The more realistic the human behaviour in the dream is, the more you cope with your loss. It is a defence mechanism and honestly, it is very common. People who have witnessed the death of say, their spouse, parents, or lovers, they see them all the time. It doesn't make you any less sane than me. And the same goes for the voices. In fact, hearing voices of a deceased is more common than you may think."

"And what about the part where Manu and I see the exact same thing, simultaneously?"

"Hmm..." hummed Dr Shukla scratching his grey sideburns, "This is where it is a little tricky. It is not very common, but there are cases where watching the same dream simultaneously has been reported by two people who love each other. It is quite rare, but not impossible. Let's try to dig deeper in the next session, okay? And if you hear the voices again, tell yourself, 'Punit is dead, there is no voice,' okay?"

Sanjana hummed and nodded. She took the prescription and shoved it in her purse. She thanked the doctor for his time, shook his rough, scaly hand and reached for the door.

"Also," announced the doctor, "You may get Manu along with you after 14 sessions. And if these pills don't work, don't lose heart, we will complement it with some other therapy. Our final resort will be to try hypnosis to assess you psychologically."

Sanjana smiled and shut the door on her way out. She paid at the reception, got her pills and left the building not feeling satisfied at all. Her house was barely 2.5 km away, so she decided to walk, to clear her thoughts. She passed a temple on her way and paused for a moment. She contemplated going inside, for the first time ever.

Sanjana had been raised as an atheist. The concept of God was just positive energy to her. She completely dismissed the idea of bargaining with God or any supreme power like you bargain while buying vegetables. She was raised to believe in herself and work hard for everything she ever wanted. If there were a God in her life, he was just a spectator.

But that day was different. She decided to pray, from outside the temple, not for her, but for Manu. She felt helpless, and she thought praying might comfort her. She prayed in her own way as if commanding the Almighty. She bowed her head once and left.

As she started back on the way to her house, her mind was distracted by the things to do after going home. She was completely unaware of the disfigured person in a dark rug that was following her from the temple.

She stopped in front of her gate to enter the security code, but suddenly, someone grabbed her hand. She jumped scared to face the person. The woman's face was dark and disfigured, with droopy eyes. She was old and had a dark, smelly rug wrapped around her. Her grip was very strong for someone her age. She looked at Sanjana and cautiously vocalised,

"I sense a strong male spirit in this house. He means no harm, but he will eventually end up harming someone by mistake. You need to salt the house to keep him out. HE is attached to your memories. You need to let him go sister before it is too late."

Sanjana jerked her hand free from the woman's grip, entered the code quickly and shut the gate immediately behind her. With feeble steps, cold hands and dry throat, she opened the door.

Manu was solving questions that Sanjana had asked him to do before she left.

"How was it?" asked Manu.

"Solve your questions first," snapped Sanjana. She wanted to avoid any conversation after the uncanny encounter outside the gate.

She went to the kitchen instead to get a glass of water. She opened the refrigerator door, bent down and fetched a cold bottle of water from the side. She drank a few sips of water and placed the bottle back.

As she closed the door of the fridge, her eyes went wide, gaze stuck at the silhouette that had formed just behind her.

"Punit is dead," she slowly whispered to herself, refusing to look back, "Punit is dead... this is not real."

"Where were you, Sanju?" she heard Punit's voice right behind her and her body was covered in chills.

Chapter 9

The ringtone of Punit's phone got lost in the loud volume of the television.

Sanjana looked keenly from the corner of her eye, knowing that the real Punit's phone was kept uncharged in his closet. Sanjana and Manu had tried countless times to open his password-protected phone in the past, but they always failed. Somehow, Sanjana completely dismissed the idea of formatting Punit's memories in the phone. There were so many photos of all of them together, as one dysfunctional but happy family.

Punit retrieved a similar looking phone from his sweatpants with his hand that looked as if it had faced the wrath of fire in the past; Sanjana continued looking in a way that Punit would not notice. She saw him look at the screen and swipe down, cancelling the incoming call. The cancelled call flashed the blurry home screen behind the pattern protected matrix. The wallpaper was hazy, but she could still deduce from the colours that it was one of the photos from when Manu was 2 years old, the exact photo that Punit's phone had back when he was alive.

After the call, Punit seemed extra jittery, but Sanjana's main concern was not that. She wanted to know who this man was, pretending to be her husband.

"I am calling an early night, Sanju," said Punit, carefully swiping his thumb across the pattern lock.

Sanjana hummed, still observing the phone screen. In moments, the phone unlocked, confirming Sanjana's wallpaper hypothesis. She was shocked to see the charlatan know so much about Punit to get every detail correctly.

Punit left the kitchen and headed upstairs dialling a number. He took a left at the end of the stairs and put the phone to his ears.

"Hello," he announced softly and disappeared into their bedroom.

Sanjana quickly grabbed her purse and let Manu out. She stuffed the crumpled paper in her purse and whispered to Manu,

"I don't know what is happening, but I want you to be strong."

She looked Manu in the eye, and he looked right back at her with the same intensity. He nodded, biting his lips as Sanjana held both of his hands.

"Is he..." Manu hesitated, "...dad?"

Sanjana shushed Manu and escorted him to the door. She wore her sandals and signalled Manu to wear his footwear. She unlocked the door and let Manu out first before getting out herself and shutting the door behind her. She buzzed the main gate open and got into her car. She instructed Manu to get in the backseat and lay low to not be seen.

"Are we running away?" questioned Manu confused lying flat between the front seat and the backseat of the car.

Sanjana started the car and chose not to turn the headlights on. She drove ahead in the direction of the open gate straight in the heart of the night as slowly as she could, trying not to make any loud noise.

"We are going to the police. I don't know who that thing inside the house is, but it not my Punit. Sure, he looks and acts like him, but I see right through him."

The car swiftly went through the gate and Sanjana took an immediate right turn.

Punit stood in the window of the bedroom with his phone pinned to his ear.

"Yes..." he spoke in baritone, "Yes... she saw the scar on my back."

He parted the curtain slowly and watched the shadow of the night sky. He kept humming on the phone. In the shadow, he saw the red taillights of Sanjana's car as she braked near the gate.

"She has just left..." he spoke again, "Nope... She did not seem alone."

Sanjana parked her car randomly on the street right near the police station. She hurried inside and asked Manu to follow her.

"Where do I register an FIR?" she asked a *havaldar*.

He directed her to a table inside the station.

Sanjana rushed to the front of the table of a police officer. The table was a mess and he was writing something on loose pieces of paper in the tube light lit station. The walls were plastered blue and the ceiling fan was barely moving. It was like an oven inside the station. The officer had two of his shirt buttons open.

"Sir... Sir, I want to file an FIR," announced Sanjana.

His head was buried in his papers. The rear end of his pen was in his mouth and he was deep in thought.

"Sit," he ordered involuntarily.

Sanjana pulled the chair in front of his desk and sat in it. Manu stood just behind her shoulder.

The policeman bent down, picked up another loose blank paper, shook the crumbs of food off the paper and laid it on his desk right at the top. He adjusted his grip on the pen and brought it close to the paper.

"Name?" he asked sternly.

"S-Sanjana Poddar."

He wrote her name on the paper shabbily and continued, "Before I file a report, I will just write rough details here and then make a detailed official copy.

"So, tell me what happened to you?"

"Sir," sighed Sanjana, "My husband... Punit, he- he died a decade ago. He was cremated publicly. And today, suddenly out of the blue, he is back."

The officer paused suddenly, almost about to drop his pen. He wiped his moustache with his other hand and continued scribbling.

"Like a ghost?" he asked.

"No, sir," interrupted Manu, "I see him too."

"He is back, sir," said Sanjana, "In the flesh."

"Shouldn't you be happy about it then?" said the policeman sarcastically, huffing under his breath.

Manu elbowed Sanjana and signalled from his eyes at the officer's paper. He had written down the words- 'Sees a ghost' and 'crazy.'

"Sir," Sanjana spat with her eyebrows clenched, "he looks like him, acts like him, talks like him and even knows the things that Punit knew, but I am certain it is not him."

The officer paused again with his face looking at the sheet and asked, "Can you produce witnesses to his cremation right now?"

"Yes," said Sanjana, "Manu, my son."

But before Manu could speak, the officer interrupted, "How old is this Manu?"

"Abhimanyu," corrected Sanjana, "Is fifteen now."

The officer immediately responded, "Which means he was five when your husband died. I cannot accept his statement; anyone else?"

Sanjana grabbed her phone from her purse and tried calling her parents. No answer.

She called Punit's parents. No answer.

The officer kept circling the word crazy with his pen.

Manu elbowed Sanjana silently yet again.

"You don't believe me, do you?" she asked spontaneously.

"I want to," said the officer, annoyed, "but listen to yourself, madam. This is impossible. Why don't you get me a death certificate and then I can consider even listening to you? Now get out of this station at once and don't waste my time."

Sanjana kicked her chair furiously and mumbled, "What was I thinking, taking help from goons!"

Manu followed her outside the station. They got into their car and Sanjana drove furiously back to their house. She parked the car inside and closed the gate.

It was late at night. She asked Manu to stand near the safe in the living room, on the table under the staircase. She went upstairs into her bedroom; Punit was asleep. She silently retrieved the key to the safe from her closet.

She hurried downstairs near Manu and opened the safe. There was another level of security digital security inside. She entered a 5-digit pin and unlocked the safe.

As she parted the tiny door open, her heart sank to the bottom of her stomach and she clutched Manu tightly.

Inside the case, on a charred and half-melted yellow folder, were the ashes of a completely burnt death certificate.

Chapter 10

The growling continued in the belly of the beast, in what seemed to her like a total eclipse. She was clawed near her neck, and fresh blood was oozing out of the open wound; what followed was a painful shriek for help from outside, Manu.

Amidst the induced blindness due to the absence of light, she frantically touched the walls to find the doorknob behind her. She turned the handle, opened the door, got out of the mist-filled room, and shut the door behind her.

She knew she was in the passage, but somehow, it seemed monstrously large. She could not guess its size in the darkness, but the spread of fog, the cold air and the expansion of her lungs made her believe that the place was not the same.

"Manu," she called, "Where are you? Beta..."

Everything had gone silent. The darkness started to lift her veil off, to show her hideous face. The eclipse was slowly passing as things became visible to her. What seemed like the passage was instead a recognized location covered in thick fog.

Among the ancient pillars, on an endless grey marble floor, stood Sanjana in her pure white saree. The horizon seemed to go endlessly around her, marking no distinction between the grey floor and the sky without a sun. In that endless nothingness, Sanjana found herself in the house of God, inside this time. She knew the temple from when she had once prayed outside. She was a visitor in that house, but the host was missing. There was no sight of the Almighty in his prosperous abode.

At the centre of the construct, however, lay a golden bell, but everything was silent, not even the slightest of the sound. The whitewashed environment of His humble house was more haunting than the dungeon of the black-veiled darkness. It appeared like death more than seeming holy.

The golden bell suddenly reverberated, comforting the hellish silence.

Sanjana looked at it. And there, near the bell, was the same old disfigured woman, in the same dark rags who had told Sanjana about the spirit in the house. She signalled Sanjana to walk close to her, with a drawstring brown pouch in her hands presenting towards Sanjana.

"You have to get rid of him," whispered the woman, but her voice echoed. She took a step towards Sanjana and continued, "You must take this salt and keep him away. Save your family."

Sanjana stared at the pouch momentarily before taking it from the putrescent hands of that woman. She drew the string and unwound it. The woman stooped and watched carefully.

"Open it and grab a fistful of salt," she instructed in her feeble, shivering voice.

Sanjana peeped inside. The grey salt belonged perfectly in the white location. She hesitated to put her hand in the pouch, breathing heavily and contemplating. Sanjana would dismiss the idea in a heartbeat if it were for herself, but when it came to Manu, she could do anything for him. She loved Manu so much that sometimes when he was not in her sight, it physically hurt her. Ever since Punit died, she tried hard to move on and be both the parents for Manu, but it was very difficult. Even when Manu got slightly hurt, it was she who wept, when he was upset, she was upset; she could even walk the ends of the earth for Manu.

Sanjana took a deep breath and grabbed a handful of salt and retrieved her hand from the pouch. She stuck her fist in front of her facing heavenwards to stop the salt from falling.

But the salt kept escaping through the gap of her hands. As it fell to the floor, the grey turned to dust.

There was an unsettling strangeness inside the closed fist. The grains of salt felt like they were hardening inside her palm. The eeriness made Sanjana open her fist.

The old woman started laughing loudly behind Sanjana, as she stood there looking at her open fist, scared stiff. On her palm, on the sticks, straws and dirt, was a single finger with an engagement ring on it and a ripped piece of red fabric that belonged to Manu's t-shirt stuck in the ring.

Sanjana dropped the contents on the floor as they turned to soil as well. The temple bell along with the woman's laughter echoed everywhere. There was nowhere to escape, no horizon to give directions, no sun in the sky to give warmth. A thick fog began to envelop her again. And among the chaos, she was waiting to hear the sound of Punit's voice. And there it was, coming from everywhere in unison. But that time, it was like a command than a voice near her ear. His voice was strong and clear-

"Cremate the boy alive!"

Sanjana gasped as her eyes widened. Her body responded in an immediate sprint. Her feet sprang to life as she lifted her saree and began running wildly like her life depended on it. Her half brain was conscious that this was just another nightmare, but she knew the ends of her nightmares turned true. She did not want to find out which part that time was going to turn into her reality.

The endless nothingness soon disappeared, and her feet started collecting dirt and gravel as she ran across the rough roads into the crematorium. She knew that it had to be the place; it had to be what Punit meant, in a way to complete a circle.

She was right, as the crematorium appeared in her field of view, covered in the same demonic fog, she immediately realised that no nightmare could be worse than that.

A five-year-old Manu was screaming for his life, tied to a big log of wood on a pyre. Near the pyre stood Punit, in a white shirt and white pyjama, with a lit torch of oil rags in his hands. He brought the flames of the torch slowly towards the pyre.

"No, dad...please, no," Manu kept screaming, "It is hurting me...Please."

Sanjana sprinted as hard as she could, but she was still far away.

"No, Punit. Stop!, she screamed at the top of her lungs.

Punit paused for a second but continued. He touched the flames to the pyre setting it ablaze.

In no time, Manu was engulfed in the hellfire screaming for help. There was no sound more painful for Sanjana than that.

She was too late. The pyre was already furiously blazing, but she jumped right in the heart of it. Punit pulled her out right back. His stronghold protected her from jumping back into it. She closed her eyes, but her tears managed to find crevices to escape. Her limbs struggled to get free, but his grip was too strong.

She cried loudly taking Manu's name.

"Don't cry, darling," said Punit holding her tightly, "He is just joining me here."

Manu shook Sanjana vigorously. She woke up, still crying loudly.

"Mom...mom," said a ten-year-old Manu, "Wake up... I am alive. Nothing has happened to me. It was a nightmare."

Sanjana looked at Manu's face sitting in his bed. She was covered in sweat and her body was burning. She cupped Manu's face and immediately realised he was very cold and shivering. She knew that he had the same nightmare.

Over the years of these shared dreams, they knew how to speak to each other and not let these nightmares affect them. Dr Shukla's pills and therapy were working. She was an irregular patient with him, but his suggestions led to fewer and fewer nightmares for her.

She put Manu back to sleep right next to her. She fondled her hand on his shoulder, humming a lullaby when suddenly she realised something strange. Manu's t-shirt had been ripped off near the sleeve; it was missing a piece of fabric.

She immediately turned on the bedside lamp to see the colour of the t-shirt. It was red.

Chapter 11

"Please come in, Ms Poddar," welcomed Dr Shukla in his sharp double-breasted blue suit that complimented his grey hair.

Sanjana entered his office, sharply dressed as well, in a black skirt complimented by the big dazzling silver jewellery and her 6-inch black pencil heels. She sat on the couch with her legs crossed right opposite to Dr Shukla's sofa-chair where he would later station himself. Her hair was neatly tucked behind her ears; her make-up was done perfectly to suit her darker skin tone.

"You look rather stunning today, Ms Poddar, haven't seen you in a while."

"Why, thank you, Doctor. I am dressed up because I am very happy."

"Would you like to tell me why?"

Sanjana leaned on the armrest of the couch and gleefully spoke, "Because of a few things. You see, I really want to thank you, doctor. Those pills and these therapy sessions have really been working very well."

"How are you doing with your nightmares now?"

"Pretty good, actually, haven't had one in a long time now. We both sleep very well. The pills and the therapy worked for sure, but you were right in telling me to follow the advice of the old woman, to salt the house."

"Correction," interrupted Dr Shukla as he opened his journal to Sanjana's section, "I simply suggesteds that if you feel that it is what will give you peace of mind, then you should do it."

"Correct," stated Sanjana, "And it did. You see, I don't believe in spirits or ghosts, good or bad, I simply don't think they can co-exist with us in the same dimensions. Salting the house simply keeps my thoughts away. Your idea of constantly reminding myself that his voice is not real was very comforting. Although, I do get the feeling of his presence at times, but not to an extent where it is hurting either of us. Thinking about the good times has helped refresh my memories. It has been months since Manu had a nightmare."

"Excellent indeed," said the doctor, "And the other?"

"I am sorry?"

"The other reason why you are so happy?"

"Oh...It is Manu's birthday today. My big boy is getting bigger and I am buying him something that he likes a lot. Right after we are done with the session, I am going shopping. We haven't really had fun for a long time now. Today is the day. But I am scared to be very happy."

"Why is that?" the doctor flipped a page and resumed writing.

"Because I think somehow, it won't last long. It just feels like at any moment, Punit may reappear and everything will be terrible again."

"Let's try creating the thought of Punit as a positive stimulus for you... like positive reinforcement."

"I don't understand you, doc."

"Positive reinforcement is rewarding a particular behaviour, so that our brain starts associating it as positive, like every time a child finishes his homework, he gets to watch the television."

"I am not a child, Dr Shukla, I cannot trick my mind into thinking something completely positive without weighing its pros and cons."

"I need you to relax and close your eyes. Let's leave the psychiatry to me for today," he smiled.

Sanjana followed his instructions and closed her eyes. He continued writing in his journal as he spoke firmly-

"From our past sessions, I know a lot about your family history. I also know the dynamics you and Punit shared before Manu came into your lives. You told me that yours was a love marriage. I want you to relax your body completely and think about the very moment you fell in love with Punit."

Sanjana's breathing was slow and controlled. She knew exactly how the sessions progressed. She was ready to tap into that memory. Her brain zoomed into its library to find the right book stored somewhere in the older bookshelves. It meticulously searched every lane to finally end up with the right book in its hands. It opened that treasure for her and started reading the memory to her like a bed-time story.

"It was our first date. Well, the first official date. We had been seeing each other for a while now, but never really went on an official date. Today was the day, September 24th. Punit texted me to meet him outside my house. When I went out, he stood there dressed in a lousy t-shirt that read 'I like donuts', which he knew was my favourite food. He had this bouquet of lilies in his hands because he knew that I hated roses.

He escorted me to his car. I was very confused about what was going on because he hadn't really told me anything. I told him to give me some time to dress up, but he denied it. I opened the back door of his car, threw my bouquet on the backseat and then sat in the front next to him. He held my hand all the time while driving. It was quite impressive how he could shift gears and steer the car safely all with just his right hand.

We parked near a park surrounded by streetlights. Inside the park, on a bench was a box of donuts that he had specially baked himself, for me. The plan was to eat those donuts on that bench, gazing at the night sky, but there were just too many mosquitoes. He always complained about how mosquitoes were naturally attracted to him because his blood type was 'A positive' and always ended up being the most bitten person, even in a group of twenty.

So, we went back to our parked car and sat inside it with the box of donuts. He switched the car yellow lights on, and we opened the box. I dug in right away, but before I could eat it, he stopped me.

He retrieved a small gift from the glove box and handed it to me saying, 'You make me feel happy'. It was a calculator; he knew that I would have hated any conventional gift. It was a perfect gift because it was so thoughtful and useful.

We began to eat later, but the moment I took the first bite, I realised that he had massively screwed up the recipe. He had put salt instead of sugar. We both laughed so hard on that, it was beautiful.

He drove me back to my house. I thanked him for the date and wished him a good night. But before I could leave the car, he said, 'I love you, Sanju. Thank you.'

In that moment, I knew I loved him back and wanted to spend my life with him.

I miss him so much. He doesn't seem capable of inflicting any harm on Manu or me. He simply can't."

Dr Shukla's phone beeped an alarm. Sanjana opened her eyes, wiping the minuscule tears off them.

"Take this thought, Ms Poddar, and use it to your advantage. Know that this person loved you very dearly and would never wish to do bad things to you or your son."

"Hush," sighed Sanjana, "Thank God for waterproof mascara."

Dr Shukla forced a smile, "I am increasing the dosage of one medication only slightly to get rid of whatever remnants are present."

Sanjana nodded and rushed to the door, "Thanks doc, but I am in a hurry today. I will buy the meds later. You may be a renowned psychiatrist, but you can never stop a woman from shopping. See you soon."

He waved at her and she rushed outside the door without paying the receptionist or without looking at anyone.

Dr Shukla buzzed the receptionist on her intercom to send his next patient. She told him that his 2:30 appointment had cancelled. So, Dr Shukla asked her to check if his 4pm could be scheduled earlier.

20 mins later, there was a knock at his door. Dr Shukla opened the door and welcomed his patient in. In came a man looking identical to Punit Poddar. Dr Shukla offered him a seat.

"First time?" he asked.

The man nodded to disagree.

"What made you change your psychiatrist?" he asked.

"Well, the previous one did not help. I hope you can."

"Name?" asked Dr Shukla, opening a brand-new journal.

"Rahul Rathod," the man replied.

Chapter 12

Sanjana rang the doorbell multiple times, but there was no answer. It seemed like her parents were not at home, neither were they answering their phones. She tried going to her in-laws' house but felt an intense sense of déjà-vu as she and Manu stood outside their gates shivering in the cold waiting for someone to answer the door.

"I think we will have to go back home," she told Manu.

Manu realised that it was the most practical thing to do. They got back in the car and went to their house.

Sanjana locked the door to Manu's bedroom from inside and slept right next to him. She was awake the whole night worrying about everything and looking out for Manu. She remembered that Dr Shukla had told her that her experience of seeing and hearing Punit was fictitious.

'Maybe Punit is real. Maybe he won't hurt Manu,' she thought.

The next morning, Manu woke up early and started preparing for his first day of tuition. Sanjana wanted him to not get intimidated by the turn of events in the house. She wanted him to be as normal as it was possible for him, given the situation.

He sat at his desk in the living room with his books open. Sanjana was preparing breakfast for him in the kitchen when Manu suddenly felt a weird aura.

Punit was at the top of the staircase, badly scratched by Poe in his sleep. He had claw marks all over his face. He was dressed in his regular office clothes leaving for work, but Poe kept hissing behind him. She clawed him whenever she got a chance. He started his descent; Manu kept looking at his face with the hair on his arms to attention. Punit chose to completely ignore him, momentarily paused near his open books and walked past him straight to the door.

"Sanju, I am off to work. I will come home early, I have a surprise for you," he announced.

Sanjana chose not to answer him and he left in silence.

Moments later, the doorbell rang.

"It might be Dr Kartik, I will buzz him in through the gate," said Manu.

Manu escorted a rather confused Dr Kartik. He insisted that he wanted to talk to Sanjana before he began teaching him. As they entered the house, Dr Kartik saw Sanjana in the kitchen and immediately sighed,

"Ms Poddar, I was trying to desperately call you last night, but your phone was not reachable."

Sanjana wiped her hands on the apron, shook his hand and apologised, "We have a bad network here, I am sorry."

"But I left you a few messages too, you should really respond. It was of prime urgency."

"Sorry again, doctor. I have about 8000 unread messages. I never read them. What happened?" asked Sanjana.

Dr Kartik explained to her how he saw a man looking like Punit enter their house last night.

Sanjana narrated to him the entire story of how shocked both were and how the police dismissed her case straightaway. She told him that she had been trying to reach her family, who was present at the funeral, but they all seem to have suspiciously disappeared and how later the death certificate was burnt last night.

"How do I prove it that we had his funeral 10 years ago?" she asked Dr Kartik desperately.

"Can't you wait till your family returns your calls?" he counter questioned her.

"What if something terrible has happened to them and we are next? We can't wait, doctor."

"You're right," he said, thinking as he stationed himself in a chair near Manu, "Neighbours?"

"It has been 10 years, everyone has moved out. To be honest, I did not even know any of them."

"Any domestic help or staff?"

"Domestic help was fired after the funeral, don't know her whereabouts and never really had security. The sad part is, Punit was so reserved that he had no friends at work either. So, the only people who attended his funeral were my parents and his parents."

Dr Kartik was stumped; he did not know how to think following that.

"I don't know how it is even possible," exclaimed Sanjana, "How did he come back? He was cremated!"

"Maybe the bodies were switched before cremation and he was always alive?" suggested Dr Kartik.

But Sanjana dismissed the idea saying, "I don't think so. I was near the corpse all the time, except for a minute or two. And even in those 2 minutes, my parents, in-laws and a bunch of guys from the crematorium were there."

Sanjana told Dr Kartik not to worry about the situation and teach Manu.

He started teaching Manu. In the meantime, Sanjana ransacked the entire house looking for clues.

After Dr Kartik went away, Manu joined Sanjana, helping her look for something that can help them prove that Punit was an imposter.

"Mom, how are you so sure that he is not dad?" asked Manu

Sanjana looked up at him surrounded by Punit's old clothes and documents lying all around their bedroom.

"I mean, he does sound and look like him. What makes you so sure?" continued Manu.

"Apart from the fact that he was cremated," said Sanjana sarcastically, "He just feels wrong."

She emphasised 'feel'. She knew it was difficult to explain, but she had known the real Punit for long enough to understand the way his touch felt, the scent of his skin, the warmth of his presence. Something there was not so right, it irked her, but she could not comprehend what exactly it was.

The front door creaked open.

"Honey, I am home," announced Punit.

Sanjana ran towards the door, Manu followed her.

Punit was standing in the doorframe holding out a bouquet of lilies dressed in a t-shirt that said, 'I like donuts.'

"What is this?" questioned Sanjana.

"Just come with me," pleaded Punit, "Please, just give me a chance. You will know."

Poe jumped into the doorframe from outside and hissed at Punit. He scared her away.

Sanjana's memory flashed to their first official date. Punit even asked her not to change and be as she was.

She grabbed the bouquet reluctantly, but half her heart was bleeding for him. How could she say no to someone who looked exactly like the love of her life? She wanted to know where this would take her. She knew, leaving Manu alone and out of her sight would be very risky, so she signalled Manu to accompany her.

She opened the backdoor of the car, let Manu inside, threw the bouquet and shut the door.

Punit sighed in disappointment.

"Fine, let's go," he grunted.

Punit had recreated their first date entirely. He had got all the details exactly. He took her to the park to the same bench as before. He specifically chose the same time as well. History repeated itself as Mother Nature got in on his grand scheme with her mosquitoes. Everything was identical as if Punit had suddenly sucked her into a wormhole and she was in her dear past- the flowers, the t-shirt, the salty donuts, everything.

Punit parked the car outside their house at the end of their date and looked at Sanjana. She knew the look from the past and her heart melted. She felt like she was falling for him all over again. She knew what he was going to say, and she dreaded it at that moment.

"I love you, Sanju. Thank you," he said.

Sanjana felt an unsettling feeling in her heart, the anomaly of it skipping a beat. She hadn't felt that way in years and today when she felt it for the stranger, it felt warm. She wanted to say that she loved him back, but she felt so guilty about it. She felt like she was cheating on the real Punit whom she loved like a moth loves the flame.

She was happy about this stranger entering her life for the first time. Her body was charged with mixed emotions of happiness, fear and guilt.

'Maybe it won't be so bad,' she thought to herself smiling, as all three of them entered the house.

Punit sat on the couch and switched on the television as Sanjana watched him smiling.

But her butterflies were short-lived, and she suddenly snapped out of the feeling as Poe crept near Punit and started cuddling him. She jumped in his lap and purred softly.

Sanjana's nostrils flared suddenly and she stormed towards Punit. Manu had seen that look on her face, he was scared, and he stepped back in silence. She threw the bouquet right in Punit's face demanding,

"Where is Poe and what have you done with her?"

Chapter 13

"Hello, maa," said Sanjana.

"Hello," said Arati, her mother-in-law, on the receiving end.

Sanjana was in a bookstore lost in a heap of academic textbooks and journals. It was Manu's 13th birthday and she wanted to gift him something meaningful, and something that he would appreciate the most. It was a celebratory moment for Sanjana, after a very long time. The mother-son pair had stopped getting the nightmares finally.

The melancholy had worn itself off and seemed to be venturing to another terrain. All the sorrow and fright had eroded in the morning sun for months now and Sanjana's life was getting back to normal. The past had drowned in a whirlpool of ecstasy after being dejected into darkness and misery for years. Punit's memories had sailed away into the end of the horizon; what remained was just fragments and faded colours.

Arati was a clinical psychologist and took great pride in her job. She was seemingly closest to Manu after Sanjana. Before Punit's demise, Manu spent hours at a stretch with his grandma listening interesting stories from her and learning from her. They were inseparable, like a little cloud in the sky, or 'sunshine' as Arati liked to call him. It was rather unusual for a kid of his age to hear stories of psychiatry, and information and theories from his grandmother. Where Manu lacked in brawns, he more than compensated in brains. It was very impressive for a four-year-old to even understand Arati's gab on behavioural identifications. But the pair seemed like they were meant for each other. No one else in the family could listen to Arati's factual conversations, and Manu needed nothing other than factual conversations.

After Punit was cremated, Arati could never find the heart to step back in the house. She had not seen Manu in a long while because he reminded her of Punit. She was still grieving and Sanjana completely understood it. She knew that if it took her that long to let go, she could not even begin to imagine how a mother would deal with the loss of her son.

"*How are you, Sanju? You sound elated...*" asked Arati.

"I am very well, maa. A quick question, the book that you and Manu always spoke about, the one that you said he should read when he is older, the one with the dreams, what is it called?"

"*The interpretation of dreams by Sigmund Freud,*" asserted Arati, "*Why? What happened?*"

"It's Manu's 13th birthday, Maa. How could you forget?"

Arati had lost track of time. In grief, they say, even friendly surroundings seem hostile and the sense of time is merely a concept. She felt extremely guilty.

"*Oh no...*" she said after a despondent sigh, "*Is today his 13th birthday already?*"

Sanjana hummed as she ransacked the bookshelves to locate the book.

"*I am terribly sorry, darling. Would you please call once you reach home? I will wish my boy.*"

Sanjana picked up the book in one hand while pressing the phone to her ear with the other.

"Oh no, you won't," she stated firmly.

Arati was taken aback.

"Because this year, you will visit him and wish him in person," continued Sanjana.

Arati hesitated before speaking, "*I...I can't...*"

"Come on, maa. It will be a nice get-together. I will call my parents too. You and papa can come by the house at 6, we will cut the cake, and we can have family dinner."

Arati paused and took a long breath. Before she could speak anything, Sanjana interrupted again amidst the voices at the cash counter, "I will not take no for an answer. Manu misses you terribly. On phone calls as well, you don't speak much with him and you've missed his birthdays. Besides, ever since his home-schooling, he has no friends at all. He is a teenager now. How long will we bury the kid in isolation? We can't let him just dwell on his father's unfortunate demise. We should at least act normal in front of him. I know that I do, but it will really be a great surprise if you come this time. He will be very happy. Please, Maa."

Arati sighed and said, "*Yes, for Manu. And don't worry, I will call your parents and invite them on your behalf. You take care of good arrangements and the feast.*"

Sanjana smiled and radiated off the love she had for her mother-in-law. Despite being from a much richer family than Punit, never once did Punit or his family ask for any money or assets from the Malhotras. The Poddars took immense pride in their profession and carried themselves with great dignity and self-respect.

Sanjana spent the afternoon shopping for the feast and gifts for Manu. Juggling with multitudinous shopping bags, Sanjana merrily walked on the street to her house humming a happy note. The family was finally moving towards a positive chapter in their lives.

In the late afternoon sun, Sanjana's house stood in the bosom of the most lavish area in the city. The tall tower of wood, glass and cement in its shallow depth of vanity, stood steadily with its whispers wasted into the Poddar garden that used to be green once. Behind the bodacious gates of the residency were cries of history trapped within the walls of the mansion. The ochre garden was hoping to now paint itself green as the wheel of time turned monstrously slowly.

But it was only about time that Sanjana would realise, that something rotten grew in that ominous garden in the womb of the night, that had only seen sorrow, distress, fear and death. The poisons that blossomed in the garden would never find their way out of the house, the poisons of death or love or betrayal or ghosts.

Sanjana stopped in front of the main gate, managing her shopping bags in her right hand to free her left. With her left hand, she reached out to the security keypad to punch in the pin. The large volume of bags got difficult for her hands and she dropped one right in front of the gate. She intended to register the key first, open the gate, pick up the fallen bag and then enter the house.

Sanjana punched in the security key carefully when the hair on her neck stood up. In the shivering light of the sun, she felt like she was being watched. The warmth of the sunlight was ironically cold.

She stood in the shadow of someone standing behind her. The gate had opened, but she froze.

The shadow slowly picked up the dropped bag and offered it to her. Sanjana remembered Dr Shukla's session and began telling herself that Punit had died and he would never hurt them. With shivering hands, she took the bag, refusing to look at the person offering it and began walking inside.

"You're welcome," said a voice sounding like Punit.

Sanjana shut the main gate without looking and stormed inside frantically whispering, "He will never hurt us... he will never hurt us... he will never hurt us."

Chapter 14

"So, Mr Rathod," said Dr Shukla as he sat across Rahul in his chair, "Could it be possible that the previous doctor couldn't help you because you wouldn't speak to him?"

Rahul kept staring at his shoes and chose not to speak anything.

Dr Shukla marked in his journal with his sharp pencil and underlined the words 'SESSION 1' the seventh time. There wasn't anything that the expert had understood from the patient beside his name and age. Every question about his family, whereabouts, diseases were left unanswered like he did not even hear them. He refused to acknowledge anything in the room or react to any of Dr Shukla's questions.

He was, in Dr Shukla's language, 'the mute patient'. The psychiatrist had dealt with many such silent cases in his career but there wasn't often just one thing that could work as a solution, so began the experimentation.

"Rahul... Can I call you Rahul?"

"Yes," whispered Rahul.

Dr Shukla looked at his wristwatch and continued asserting, "Rahul, it has been 20 minutes and you have sat here in absolute silence. Now, I know a lot is going in your head, but if you really want to not repeat the same mistake you did with your previous doctor, and want me to help you, you must speak to me. Do you understand me, Rahul?"

He kept looking at his shoes and moments later, shifted his gaze to the doctor's desk.

"Okay, Rahul, don't answer me in words or sentences, but just nod if you feel like it, okay?"

Rahul nodded, still looking at the desk. His eyes were weary and red like he had not slept in days. Dark circles around his eyes stood out on his fair but dirty skin. His beard was unruly, and his hair looked like had not been trimmed for months.

"Have you not slept well?"

Rahul nodded twice, steadily; Dr Shukla noted in his journal.

"Since how long haven't you slept?"

There was no response from the receiving end of the question.

"Is something bothering you?"

He moved his head to the window and slowly nodded.

Dr Shukla knew he had to throw in a list of possible causes of his disturbed behaviour and look closely for a shift in his body language to understand what really was bothering Rahul.

"Is it your job or sex or a fight or a relationship or loss or money..."

Rahul had never made eye contact with the doctor, but at the sound of the word relationship, his bloodshot eyes stared directly into the eyes of Dr Shukla. A nerve was pressed, Rahul had reacted. His body experienced tremors in his muscles. He gulped and whispered, looking back at his shoes,

"Yes... I have been depressed for a long time because of that. It feels like everyone I love and care for goes away from me. You see, I did something terrible and I want to run away from it. Start fresh. But these dark thoughts keep appearing again and again, and I know, I will do the terrible thing again."

The room got engulfed in lingering silence. Dr Shukla keenly observed Rahul's movement, but he did not give anything away through his body language. Like a seasoned veteran, he controlled his fits himself without moving much and kept staring into nothingness.

Dr Shukla looked at his watch and quickly scribbled the words- money, relationship, darkness, did something terrible and what he wrote in all capitals and circled it was the word- GUILT.

The alarm on the doctor's phone shattered the silence in the room. Before the doctor could say anything, Rahul stood up and said, "Thank you, any pills?"

Dr Shukla closed his journal and stood up to see Rahul as a completely different person than the one during the session. He seemed more confident like he had vanquished his demons in that 40minutes long unfruitful session. Like the silence in which the pair stood, communicated more to Rahul, than the vocabulary that the doctor sought.

"None," said the doctor brushing off his vest and walking towards his desk.

Rahul stationed himself across his doctor. Dr Shukla carefully placed his journal in the desk drawer, locked it with a key and placed the key in the top drawer.

"Rahul, I don't think you need any medications, yet," suggested Shukla, "I think therapy will suffice for you. But to do that, I need your cent per cent co-operation. You will have to speak to me, and not just in nods, okay?"

Rahul stood up to shake hands with Dr Shukla and leave as he nodded.

Dr Shukla stood up, handed him a ticket that he needed to show at the reception for his next appointment and pay the fees for this one.

"Do you have insurance?"

"No, sir, do I look like I have insurance? I may not have money, but I will pay for this therapy."

"See, Rahul," stated Dr Shukla, "Just for the sake of not wasting your money, promise me you will open up in our next session."

As Rahul held Dr Shukla's hand in his own, he gloved his hand with the other tightening his grip and saying,

"Let me warn you, doctor if you wish to take a plunge into the dark, be prepared to get lost."

He paid at the reception, booked his next appointment and left.

He lit up a cigarette and started smoking it, wandering in the streets near Dr Shukla's facility. It all seemed so mundane to him, the happy faces of the people, their attires and makeup like it was all a facade to hide their ugliness, to conceal their filth, to mask their darkness. In a wisp of smoke, it would all be revealed, and the entire town will be painted in the shades of unholy white, he thought.

His thoughts brought him wandering in front of a house that stood apart from the rest of the neighbourhood. In the lavish riches of that area, that mansion embarrassed the inferior jewels of the rest.

He stood across the street facing the house with the cigarette held between his blackened fingers. In front of the main gate was a scrumptious woman dressed all in black struggling with numerous shopping bags.

Rahul took a last fag, dropped the bud to the floor and stubbed it out as she dropped one bag down. He crossed the street and picked up the bag. He saw her punch '46752' at the security gate. He held out the bag for her, but she refused to look at him. She grabbed the bag as the gate opened.

"You're welcome," said Rahul thinking of her as a spoilt rich snob.

She ran inside, screaming, "He will never hurt us..." repetitively and she shut the gate without even looking at him, leaving a confused Rahul outside the main gate.

Rahul dialled a number on his phone, a woman answered on the other end.

"Hello...I will be late," he said intensely, "I have got some research to do," and he hung up.

Chapter 15

It was 6:30 a.m. and the sun was still waking up. Mugdha stood outside the Poddar residence, waiting for the gate to open. She tried ringing the bell many times but there was no answer from inside. She unlocked her phone and dialled Sanjana's number. She wasn't feeling very positive about Sanjana answering her phone, but she wanted to give it a last chance before attempting to forcefully enter inside. Her premonitions were correct; Sanjana did not answer her phone.

Mugdha looked around if somebody was watching her and she confirmed that no one was. She opened the text message from Sanjana that said-

'Money transferred. Freezer. Help me. Come Now!! 46752'

Mugdha punched in 46752 as the security key to the gate. She entered inside loudly, announcing herself.

"Sanjana ma'am, it's me, Mugdha."

She was careful enough not to be so loud as to wake the neighbours. The last thing she wanted was somebody to see that she was snooping around. She also wanted to keep at complete discretion that Sanjana had called her to do detective work to prove that Punit was an imposter.

"Ma'am, I've come for your office work," she announced not very loudly, "I understand it's urgent... you had called... ma'am."

She walked slowly through the front yard to finally pause before the door. She knocked at the door and realised it was already ajar. She knew that she had to get in because the message sounded very important. It seemed like Sanjana's desperation for help was put into one text message.

Mugdha gulped the freshness of the morning as she entered inside to what she could only imagine as her worst nightmare.

"Ma'am," she announced herself, carefully clutching the pepper-spray inside her purse," I let myself in. Hello, is anyone there?"

The mansion that basked in its pulchritude from outside looked like a dive into the darkness from inside. The house, if it was one, was an absolute mess. It looked like the place had been ransacked like the abode was raped. Nothing was in its place, broken items of showpieces were on the floor, shattered TV screen, utensils on the floor, clothes of a child on the staircase, spilled soup across the floor and a putrescent stench that made Mugdha gag.

She wore a pair of rubber gloves and covered her nose with a handkerchief. She carefully placed each step, trying not to move anything on the floor. The bathroom door was open; she went in. It was spotless unlike the rest of the house, no damage, nothing moved.

She came out and looked around when her gaze got transfixed at a hammer at the end of the staircase. She manoeuvred her way through the mess of what looked to her like Manu's old clothes to inspect the weapon.

She leaned in to touch the hammer, other than the rusty appearance, it felt to her like she had found the prime weapon of destruction in the house. What she did not know was if the destruction was the only thing that happened a few hours ago, or if there was more in store for her, she was about to find out.

Near the hammer was a small, yet prominent trail of blood that began at the top of the staircase, with a noticeable volume, and disappeared midway to Manu's bedroom. Mugdha followed where the trail led her, into the kid's bedroom.

The opened door revealed the violence that the room had witnessed. Every single item was shattered except the lights. The mattress was flung, every piece of cloth in the closet was out, the wooden cabinets were broken, Manu's books were all across the room, pieces of blank papers from his notebook torn across the floor, the mirror was shattered, and the broken pieces of glass carpeted the floor reflecting Mugdha' s frightened distorted image.

'That poor child,' she thought.

She entered Sanjana's bedroom to see a similar construct but not as bad as Manu's bedroom. The cabinets were similarly ransacked but not completely. The window was broken, and the gaping hole looked like something had been thrown out of it.

Mugdha went downstairs dreading the olid air that seemed to grow stronger as she approached to inspect the last room left in the house, the kitchen.

She crossed the dining table to enter the kitchen. The table still had soup floating on it, with chunks of meat suspended on top. As she entered the kitchen, the stench involuntarily had her elbow covering her nose and the moment she realised why, she knew why Sanjana had paid her so much of money.

The kitchen floor was a cesspool of fresh blood, puddles of it across the floor. Mugdha could not bear it any more, she rushed to the sink to vomit, with flooded eyes and body drenched in sweat. She wiped her face with the handkerchief she had covered her nose with, ready to vomit in the sink, but the sink had no place for her spew, it had already hosted its inhabitants- A thick lining of blood and hair and something that stuck near the drain, an eye.

Mugdha ran out of the kitchen into the clean bathroom and puked. She sat on the floor near the commode shivering with fright, barely even able to move. Pearls of perspiration gathered on her forehead and trickled down her temples. Her wet eyes, runny nose and shivering chin signalled her that this was not a solo job.

With trembling hands, she took her phone out of her purse and dialled a number after waiting for an eternity of ringtone, he answered.

"Hello, Nipun?"

"*Mugdha, what time is it?*" said Nipun sounding still sleepy.

"It's early, I am sorry, but I did not know what to do," said Mugdha shaking badly in her boots.

"*What's.... what's the matter? Is everything alright?*"

"Nipun, I am at Poddar's place, remember Sanjana, I spoke about her."

"*Oh yes, the crazy daughter of that industrialist who is paying you crap loads of money. Who thinks her husband is back from the dead? What are you doing there so early?*"

"She texted me last night, Nipun, said it was urgent, and I..." she began sobbing, "And... I had slept and got it this morning... and I don't know what has happened here, Nipun."

Nipun suddenly woke up like a shot of caffeine was injected in him.

"*What's going on, Mugdha?*"

"Someone was killed here last night, Nipun, and the house is completely empty. From the looks of it, it seems like there wasn't even a police case."

"*Just like that woman Sanjana had said? The police are involved in this or bought?*"

"I don't know, I just went into the kitchen and it is a bloodbath. The sink even has hair and an eye in it."

"*What the hell, Mugdha, get out right now.*"

"Please stay on the phone, I have to do one last thing before I get out."

Mugdha got up from the bathroom floor, flushed her vomit, emptied her bottle of perfume on the handkerchief, tied it to the nose and marched into the kitchen again.

"*What are you doing?*"

"Her message said something about the freezer."

She opened the freezer and found a balled-up piece of paper in it.

"I found a piece of paper in it, Nipun."

"*What does it say?*"

She opened the piece of paper; it seemed old and faded through years, like it was accidentally washed as it hid in the pockets of clothing. But few things were clearly legible on that piece of paper.

"It's a payment receipt of a 'Sai Crematorium'. The dates and everything is faded, the age is only slightly faded, there are 2 numbers it looks like 35 or something. I am sure for the 5, the 3 could be 3 or 5. The name of the deceased is half faded too... There's a 'dar' at the end."

"*Age 35, Punit-freaking-Poddar,*" gasped Nipun, "*And we thought Sanjana was crazy. She has proof.*"

"Help me in this case, Nipun, I will split the money, can't do this alone. Someone died here last night."

"*Meet me at the Sunshine Cafe in 20 minutes, bring this note,*" Nipun completed.

Chapter 16

"Come in, Rahul," invited Dr Shukla in his double-breasted grey suit.

Dr Shukla had a very neat fashion sense. He would always wear tailored-fit three-piece suits with a striking tie. His suits would either complement his salt and pepper look or would harmonise with the elegant tan furniture. He was rather fit for his age and pulled off certain bold colour choices really well.

It was Rahul's eighth session and he had begun to realise that Dr Shukla had never repeated any piece of clothing ever, not even his shoes. Not that Rahul was keenly observant, but there was nothing else they did in those sessions than silently observe.

'The mute patient' had shown no progress whatsoever. Each session, Rahul showed up on time, sat in front of his psychiatrist and never responded to any question. Dr Shukla's therapy had practically regressed as Rahul had stopped nodding as well. He silently sat with a forced smile stuck on his face as Dr Shukla asked him even the most basic questions.

Like always, without a word, Rahul sat in his regular spot across the doctor. Dr Shukla had tried several methods that had historically worked, but Rahul refused to respond to any of the methods. Dr Shukla was running out of patience and Rahul was running out of time.

"Rahul..." explained the doctor, "It is not like you don't understand. I know you do, so you need to start talking to me. I have explained to you again and again how these sessions work. I have tried to establish friendly conversations. I have tried to ask you completely neutral questions. You won't even tell me how your day was. To be honest, I don't think I can help you."

Rahul kept silently looking at Dr Shukla's shoes without uttering any form of sound.

Dr Shukla sighed.

"Let me tell you a story from when I was a kid..." Dr Shukla tried to start a conversation like always.

Rahul twitched his neck and looked away.

'Some progress- negative body language' wrote the doctor in Rahul's case journal.

Rahul yawned loudly and Dr Shukla was taken aback. Never once in his career did a patient yawn before him that was not a part of the therapy.

"What is it, Rahul? Am I boring you?"

Rahul's muscles got taut and he looked up in one corner, still avoiding eye contact.

"Okay, let me tell you some interesting stories then. Well, you seem like a person who would take an interest in someone else's life, don't you?"

His muscles began to relax, his neck started to shrink into his shoulders and his eyes began moving towards Dr Shukla. The psychiatrist scribbled untidily in his notes.

"Rahul," said Dr Shukla very softly, "Did you hear about that woman who sees her dead husband?"

Rahul inhaled loudly; Dr Shukla scribbled- 'Almost eye contact.'

"She is this rich woman living as a single parent, her assets all in the name of her son after he turns eighteen. She thinks her dead husband is haunting her. Ridiculous you may think, but I don't find it humorous at all."

Rahul's eyes widened, nostrils flared, pursed lips and he made eye contact.

"Now," Shukla chose to continue, "She used to compete in javelin throw in her school days. So, in her therapy sessions, we are actually playing a miniature version of javelin throw to calm her nerves, to distract her from getting such dark thoughts. And you know how I could help her? It was because she has told me everything about her. Everything."

Rahul kept looking at the doctor's eyes like he was staring into his soul.

"Your turn, Rahul," asserted Dr Shukla, "What's your story?"

Rahul exhaled loudly and broke his eye contact, back to staring at his shoes.

"My depression has brought this strange darkness in me, doc," whispered Rahul for the first time in seven sessions.

But Dr Shukla's success was short-lived as the story ended with just that sentence.

"Show me your darkness, Rahul," said Dr Shukla, "I won't judge. It is my job. Speak to me."

"I am... not... comf-comfortable", stuttered Rahul, "This room... th-these walls, they are so unfriendly. They are... eating me up, consuming me in wrath."

Dr Shukla cocked his head at Rahul's strange choice of words, but what he said next was music to Rahul's ears.

"Why don't you befriend the room then?"

Rahul swayed his feet slightly without looking at Dr Shukla or saying anything.

Dr Shukla looked at his watch and said, "We still have about 7 minutes and frankly therapy will be much effective if we just get this done. Why don't I step out for the rest of the session, and you speak to the walls and befriend this space? Capisce?"

Rahul got up and exclaimed, "You think I am crazy!"

"I don't think anyone is 'crazy', that's kind of my job," finished Dr Shukla and stepped out.

Rahul looked around and waited for a moment before springing into action. He marched directly towards Dr Shukla's desk. He opened the top drawer surreptitiously without making any sound. There it was, resting among some intellectual documents, the literal key to his friendship with the room, longing to be held by him, longing to blossom with his greed. He unlocked the bottom cabinet with the key to a limitless treasure of detailed patient journals. In the towers of that blue and white, a distinct journal tarnished the laws of gravity through the hands of a sinner, the journal that bore the title- 'Sanjana Poddar.'

Rahul stared into his menacing darkness as he retrieved his phone from his pockets and clicked pictures of every page of that journal from the beginning of time.

He carefully placed everything back to where it was without making any sound. He swiftly moved away from the desk and began to go out of the office when he bumped into Dr Shukla in the doorframe.

"Befriended the room?" Dr Shukla smiled.

Rahul nodded slowly and silently, still looking down and shivering. He began to leave when the doctor said out loudly,

"We all have darkness in us, Rahul. But just remember that the path to Hell is paved with good intentions."

Chapter 17

Sanjana knew something was wrong with Poe. The cat that scratched the Punit just this morning, was now cuddling with him, purring all around him begging for scratches on her back.

Manu and Sanjana both stood in the kitchen as they saw how their aggressive kitten had suddenly become docile.

"Mum, do you think he did something to Poe?" whispered Manu.

Sanjana held Manu's shaking hand. He feared his father due to the nightmares he and Sanjana shared. The premise was always such that it seemed like Punit wanted to hurt Manu.

The only real memory of his father, or at least the one he thought that felt the most real, was worse than his nightmares. He could only remember his father's image as the man with a hammer wanting to take his life, while he and his mother were trying not to breathe loudly in the kitchen cabinet.

"Manu, go try to make conversation with him. Try to understand his body language and see if he is lying about anything," instructed Sanjana.

Manu looked at her, trying to process what she had just asked of him. He was always scared of his father, and now his mother wanted him to speak to this man on their couch.

"Mum..." Manu hesitated, "I think Poe identified the scent of dad. Which is why she behaved erratically ever since this other dad came to the house. Is it possible that when we went out with him on your date, someone may have come inside and switched our cats?"

Sanjana looked at Manu. His theory made perfect sense. It was very likely that if Punit or whoever this person was, knew everything in so much details, he was being accompliced by someone else.

"Manu, please baby," pleaded Sanjana, "If we really want to expose this man, you will have to help me. We need to wait until he makes a mistake which gives him away."

Manu bit his lower lip, hummed in acceptance and started walking toward his dad and Poe.

"Shh..." Sanjana hissed from behind, "I am right here, don't be scared."

While Manu did not know if the person on their couch really was his father or not, but one thing he knew was that his father was dead for 10 years and he had attended his funeral. There was no conceivable way that he could have come back from the dead. He had to prove it, not for himself but for his mother.

Manu sat in silence in the armchair beside the couch. Poe was in Punit's lap, gently purring while he watched the television.

Sanjana desperately dialled Arati's number again hoping to get through. The phone rang, and Arati answered.

"Hello- hello, maa?" Sanjana said breathlessly.

"*What happened, beta?*"

"Maa, get here right now, it is urgent. I cannot explain on the phone."

"Sanju, you are scaring me. Is everything alright? Something happened to you or..."

"Maa, listen to me," Sanjana interrupted, "The signal is weak in the house, come here right now!"

"I can't understand you, beta. Hello... I can't hear... hel- hello."

The phone got disconnected. Sanjana checked her mobile network, there were no bars. She connected the phone to the WIFI and sent Arati a chat message-

'Come home ASAP!!'

She saw a single grey tick beside her message.

As she waited for the double blue tick, her attention was caught by Manu trying to make conversation with Punit. She did not want to get closer to raise any alarms, so she just observed.

She could see the back of Punit's head and the side of her son's face. His lips were vehemently moving amidst the loud sound of the television, his body language seemed confrontational. If she could understand from reading his lips, she guessed Manu had just said,

"Where had you disappeared for 10 years then?"

There were very slim chances that Arati would even read the text, given that it was very late at night and texting was the last thing expected from Sanjana. She just hoped that Arati would read the message and get to her house and help her expose the stranger.

Manu got back to the kitchen with his palm wrapped around his wrist.

"What... what did he do?" said Sanjana enraged.

"He didn't do anything," said Manu, "It was Poe. She scratched me."

Sanjana frowned with annoyance. Poe, though was aggressive, had never scratched Manu before. Sanjana stepped a foot towards Punit, but Manu stopped her.

"It is okay, mummy," he consoled her, "Let's go to my room, I will tell you what I observed."

Manu grabbed a few slices of bread from the fridge and ran straight to his room; Sanjana followed.

He ate some bread pieces on the way to his room and sat on his bed. Sanjana locked the door behind her.

He tossed her the remaining slices and said, "I don't want dinner, I feel full."

"What happened with that man?" Sanjana enquired.

"He is unreadable, mother. His body language was practically non-existent. Although he still seems like he doesn't like me, just based on that, I would say he is dad."

"Did you ask him why now?"

"I did ask him where he was all this time if he was alive."

"And…" interrupted Sanjana.

"And then Poe scratched me."

Sanjana got startled by the doorbell. She asked Manu to lock himself from inside as she ran down.

Sanjana opened the door, it was Arati. She hugged her tightly and teared up.

"What's the matter, beta?" asked her mother-in-law, "You seemed troubled on the phone, so I came straight away."

Sanjana grabbed Arati by the wrist, forced her into the living room near the couch and pointed at Punit.

"This," she exclaimed, "This is the reason why I called."

Arati looked at Punit as he got up and said, "Mom, what are you doing here so late?"

Arati looked at Sanjana with sad eyes and said, "Now what did he do to upset you?"

It felt like Sanjana's heart had been ripped off her chest.

"M-Maa," stammered Sanjana with sweat on her upper lip, "Aren't you..sur-surprised to see him?"

"Why surprised?" smiled Arati, "Where do you think he made the donuts for you today?"

Arati sat beside Punit on the couch as Poe jumped right back in Punit's lap. It was as if this man had done some kind of black magic on everyone.

"The funeral, maa," yelled Sanjana tearing up.

"I don't want to talk about it, Sanju," said Arati sternly and looked at Punit.

The mother-son began chatting in no time, leaving an angry Sanjana to herself, letting her think that she is going crazy.

Sanjana quickly dialled her father-in-law's number. He answered the phone. Sanjana explained him the situation and said that Arati had not reacted to it at all. She even refused to speak about the funeral.

"What funeral are you talking about, beta?"

"Ten years ago, papa. We cremated Punit publicly, in front of you, in front of me!"

"You must be kidding," he laughed, *"I don't get the joke, but there was no funeral."*

And he hung up.

As Sanjana turned around, Arati stood in the doorframe waving her goodnight. Punit escorted her to the main gate.

Sanjana stood in the middle of her house, eyes drowning in tears, feeling completely helpless. She dialled her parent's house, but no one answered the phone.

Her teary eyes met Manu at the top of the staircase. She opened her mouth to speak, but Manu interrupted, "I heard."

He hugged Sanjana and said, "Mom, I swear, whoever is involved in this will pay."

Sanjana wiped her tears quickly. She was not weak. She had to be strong for both of them.

"Now, mom," said Manu, "I know you are a hoarder and you have even the smallest piece of paper saved."

"Where are you getting at son?"

"Is it possible that you may have some kind of payment receipt or something from the crematorium?"

Sanjana's body was covered in goosebumps, she knew of a receipt from the Sai crematorium was somewhere in the house. All she had to do was find it.

"I will look for the receipt elsewhere," said Sanjana, "you look in your room and lock it from inside. We don't want to take any risks and give the notion to this man that we are on to him. Behave normally."

Manu agreed and went into his bedroom.

Punit entered the house with a cocky smile swept across his face. Sanjana balled up her fist with anger, her teeth gritting.

"Your phoney charm will not work with me," she said, "Where the hell is my cat?"

Punit ignored.

"Answer me!" she demanded, "What have you done with Poe. What spell do you have your parents under? What the hell have you done with my parents?"

Sanjana grabbed things from the kitchen and started throwing them.

"Calm the hell down, Sanju!" said Punit, but she kept throwing utensils.

In that chaos, his phone sprang to life. It was the same secretive call that he had received earlier too.

Punit looked at his phone screen and swiftly moved upstairs.

Sanjana purposely did not follow him immediately to not raise suspicions.

She went upstairs after some time to hear Punit's conversation with the mystery caller from outside the door.

"The plan is working..." said Punit in a whisper, "We are in stage 2 now. It is just a matter of weeks or months till we reach stage 5 and then Manu will be gone forever."

Sanjana's heart was in her mouth. There was nothing more important to her than Manu's well-being. She was fuming with anger. First, this man claims to be her beloved husband and now he wants to murder her child.

Sanjana marched downwards in anger and went straight into the kitchen.

Manu searched his room everywhere but found nothing. He heard noises of utensils from downstairs, but he did not dare to go down. There was a lot of chaos in the passage outside his room, but he wanted to focus on finding what was important and search his room again.

Half his heart was worried for his mom and other of his heart was respecting her order to stay locked in his room. He heard a lot of items shifting in the kitchen again. The world outside seemed to be in a complete state of chaos.

Sounds of utensils, Poe's scary monstrous cries, footsteps in the passage, doors banging. Manu had had enough. He opened the door and was ready to go down when he saw Punit look at him from the top of the staircase descending.

Punit descended the stairs where he met Sanjana. She smiled at him and said, "I am sorry for my behaviour. You know how I overreact sometimes?"

Punit raised his eyebrow.

"Let's just forget what happened and come sit with me. I made you dinner while you were on that long call."

Manu's breath shivered at the top of the stairs. He could not guess what was happening.

Sanjana looked like a complete mess. Her dupatta was missing, her hair was in all directions, she was profusely sweating, and her eyes reflected darkness that Manu had never seen before.

"Go to your room!" she commanded Manu as her voice monstrously echoed in the mansion.

Manu ran into his room.

Punit sat at the dining table ornamented with a big covered cauldron at the centre and a small soup bowl, also covered, in front of him.

Sanjana lovingly took a napkin and placed it on Punit's lap and said, "Bon appétit, darling."

Punit smiled, "And you? Aren't you dining with me?"

"I am full, from the lovely date we had," she said, kissing his ear from behind, "Why don't you start?"

Punit tucked himself comfortably in his chair and lifted off the plate covering his soup bowl. As the hot vapour effervesced, Punit gagged of the strong smell.

"Honey, what happened?" asked Sanjana innocently grabbing his shoulders tightly.

"Honey," said Punit trying not to puke, "I think the chicken has gone bad."

Sanjana grabbed him even more tightly and rubbed her nose on his earlobe sensuously, and said,

"Oh, poor baby, it's not chicken. It's your blood cat!"

Chapter 18

"Sanjana," growled Punit getting up, with his hands covering his mouth, "tell me that you're joking."

"Husband dearest," said Sanjana with an uncanny calmness, "You think you can fool everyone, but not this house."

Punit's face got red with anger as she spoke.

"We see right through you, you imposter," insinuated Sanjana, "I see it, Manu sees it and Poe saw it too."

Punit brought his shivering hands to his forehead and pulled his hair back with extreme rage.

"You have no idea," he said with his voice vibrating in his throat like it would explode any moment, "You have no idea, woman, what you have done."

He smashed the ceramic soup bowl on the floor and swept the cauldron across the table. There was cat soup everywhere.

Sanjana did not calculate that this man would become so violent. She stood still looking him in the eye, trying to gauge his next move.

Manu heard the pandemonium and was scared for his mother. He knew her anger and from the past, he knew his father's anger too, if he was Punit. They would never survive the night if something was not done. But if he was even seen between them, it was very likely that Manu would become collateral and this Punit, his father or not, would not even care if he hurt Manu.

Completely unaware of the telephonic conversation, Manu had to ensure that his mother was safe. He did not know how to forgive himself if something were to happen to his mother.

He got out of his room, tiptoeing around the corner, stepping on every step carefully without making any sound. His parents were not in his field of view.

'They might be in the kitchen,' he judged by direction from where the loud arguments were born.

He heard the kitchen cabinet open.

"Choose your next words very carefully," his mother threatened, "Threaten me, and I will let it pass but threaten my child, you will wake something in me that you will not be able to control."

He heard a loud bang. He did not dare go into the kitchen.

"You are doing all this for Manu?" yelled his father, "You killed an animal..."

Another loud bang.

"I am just seeking blood for blood," he finished with another loud thud.

Manu gasped and turned around to run.

Punit paced towards the kitchen, stepping in the muck of the cat stew.

"Where do you think you are going?" Sanjana followed Punit.

He saw the kitchen from its point of entry, and he hesitated. There was blood everywhere, small puddles of it from the floor to the sink. The bloody knife lay next to the sink with the cabinet below wide open. The cabinet housed the kitchen trashcan which was now spilling with the mutilated black and grey cat. Half the cat's body was out with its legs missing.

Punit ran and closed the sink cabinet when he noticed his razor blade that Sanjana might have used to shave off the cat's fur. In the sink, was the remnants of that fur and an eye.

Punit was careful not to touch anything and brought his tremored hands to his temples as Sanjana stood across the kitchen looking at him.

"You think you are so smart," she vocalised, "But we all know you are a fake."

Punit looked at her, his vein on the forehead ready to pop.

"You think I don't know about your secret calls? Well, I do…" she pushed him more, "And whatever do you mean by stage 2."

"I don't know what you're talking about," lied Punit.

"I don't know what you are talking about," she mimicked him in a shrill voice, "I don't expect to hear the truth from you, you sick vermin," she continued, "But one thing is for sure, whatever that stage 5 you were referring to, you will never be able to hurt Manu."

Punit marched towards the kitchen cabinet.

"Oh yes? And who will stop me?" he asked

"Oh yes…and who will stop me?" she mimicked him again aggressively.

"Stop it!"

"Stop it!"

"You can't even prove that your husband died," he stated.

Sanjana was flabbergasted, she had no response.

"Who will believe you?" he scoffed, "Not even the woman who is closer to you than your mother. And Manu… he… ends… today!" he finished dramatically.

He opened the kitchen cabinet and grabbed a familiar hammer from it.

Sanjana stood across the room, looking at him, fuming in wrath.

"Choose your next words very carefully," she alarmed him, "Threaten me, and I will let it pass but threaten my child, you will wake something in me that you will not be able to control."

Punit banged the hammer against the cabinet. Sanjana got startled.

"You are doing all this for Manu?" yelled his father, "You killed an animal..."

He tossed the hammer in the air, caught it back and swung it like a bat against the wall.

"I am just seeking blood for blood," he raised his eyebrows and finished with another loud thud.

Sanjana inhaled shaking breaths as her tender heart paced rapidly. A lot had happened that night which she never imagined would happen.

Punit ran with the hammer into the living room, sprinting upstairs.

"No more Manu after today," he announced satanically.

Sanjana sprinted behind him as fast as she could. She caught onto his foot before he could take a right turn to go to Manu's bedroom.

"Lock the door," she yelled.

Punit grabbed her shoulder-length ebony hair and banged her head on the floor.

"This ends tonight!" he announced wickedly.

Sanjana scraped her forehead on the floor and started bleeding profusely. Her locomotor sensors had given up and she was unable to move. Her blood oozed out of her forehead to the floor. She dragged her body to Manu's bedroom behind Punit, her eyes flooding, her heart sinking in her chest.

"Please," she cried, "Please...don't."

Punit kicked the door to Manu's room open and entered with the hammer in his hand and anger in his eyes. Sanjana had dragged herself only halfway through the passage. She was frantically trying to get up, but she could move only slightly.

Her helpless self began wailing as she heard Punit scream his name followed by a heart wrenching loud thuds.

Every thud of the hammer was like a punch in her chest. She clawed her way back to strength as she got back up on her feet.

Punit came out, breathing heavily with the hammer slacking from his left hand.

"Where is he?" he demanded.

Sanjana quickly realised that Manu may have heard the commotion and ran somewhere else. He was a smart boy, but the man posing as his father had lost complete control.

Sanjana turned around and ran for her life into her bedroom across the passage.

"Where the hell is he?" demanded Punit even more angrily.

Sanjana locked the bedroom door behind her and realised that Manu was not there. But she knew that Punit did not know it and keeping him around the bedroom meant buying Manu some time to escape.

She saw Punit's locked phone on the bed, she dialled 100 on the phone.

"Please… please come quickly. There is an intruder in the house, and he is trying to kill us."

Sanjana gave the complete address and the security code to the policeman on the other end of the phone before she hung up in fear.

She started emptying Punit's closet, pretending that she is making Manu some space to hide. As she moved the clothes, she realised that her vision had started to get blurry due to her concussion.

Punit banged the door with the hammer loudly.

"You can't hide forever," he screamed.

Sanjana kept removing everything from his closet to make it look genuine if he entered inside. She only hoped that the police arrive before he realises it.

She did not want him to realise that she had called the police, so she threw his phone through the glass window, breaking it in the process.

As she ransacked the documents in the drawer, she found a rather peculiar paper that she knew she had seen before. It looked faded as if it was accidentally washed with laundry. It read 'Sai Crematorium'.

There was another loud thud on the door and the intruder was inside. Sanjana quickly balled the receipt and put it in her mouth. She swiftly closed the closet and stood in front of it to guard it and make it look more genuine.

Punit jumped in front of her, held her by the shoulder and threw her near the door in one single blow.

Sanjana quickly moved out of the door, slammed it shut and latched it from outside.

She knew Manu was hiding in the bathroom, as that was the only place left for him to hide.

She rushed downstairs as she spat the ball of paper in her hands. She knew she did not have much time, but she wanted to make sure that Manu was safe.

She was losing consciousness fast. She ran to the mess in the kitchen and grabbed her phone from the counter. She opened it, pressed some keys as her phone chimed. She immediately texted a contact named 'Mugdha Case'.

'Money transferred. Freezer. Help me. Come Now!! 46752'

She heard Punit from above trying to come out. Her vision blurred further, and her eyelids started to get heavy. She opened the freezer and put the balled-up paper inside.

She ran to the kitchen cabinet and retrieved a miniature javelin out of it. She rushed to the bathroom door holding it in defence.

"Baby, you are in there?" she asked pausing in front of the bathroom door.

"Mom," said Manu from inside, unlocking the door to get her in, but it was too late.

Punit had already sprung out their bedroom and sprinted down.

Sanjana closed the slightly open bathroom door and said,

"Stay inside, Manu. Keep it locked."

Punit paused on the stairs facing Sanjana, with his hammer raised, about 20 feet away from her.

"Step aside!" he commanded.

Sanjana stepped in front of the bathroom, latched the door from outside as she heard a distant police siren.

"The police will be here in no time, you don't want to do this," she said, knowing that she could collapse any moment.

"By the time they reach here, it will all be over," he asserted.

He was not wrong, the siren seemed very far away. There were still many barriers to cross before they came inside.

Punit took one step towards Sanjana and she stretched her javelin behind her shoulder.

"Fair warning, stranger," she sounded sinister, "I will pierce your flesh if you try to hurt my son and I have never missed."

Punit contemplated for a moment as she looked him in the eye. He tossed his hammer from his left to his right.

The siren grew louder.

He took one step ahead.

"Not... my...child," she said, "Not today."

And threw the javelin straight at him. The javelin forced its projectile right into the tender flesh of his left thigh. He tossed the hammer up and collapsed on the step screaming in pain.

"You were warned, outsider," she said with a shivering breath as her eyes started to close.

The front door broke open as a bunch of policemen came storming inside with their guns cocked. One of them was the same guy Sanjana had met at the station.

She was relieved momentarily before Punit yelled,

"Officers, get her… she hurt me. Look."

Sanjana started shaking her head side to side, trying to say that she had called for help.

"I called you from my phone, but she snatched it and pretended she needed help. She is mad, take her away. She even killed the cat in the kitchen."

Sanjana's eyes were closing. She knew exactly how the blame was falling on her as she saw the familiar police officer whispering to Punit indistinctly.

She opened the bathroom door to check on Manu before her lights were out. The police were closing in. The bathroom door opened to an empty bathroom and an open window. Manu had escaped.

"Call the asylum," she heard the familiar officer say before she passed out.

~

As she opened her eyes, all she saw was darkness. She felt claustrophobic and motion-sick. She tried to move but realised that she was restrained in a jacket sitting upright at the back of a very slow-moving van.

Flashes of lights slowly passed through the van window, to acclimatise her to the faces of the people from the asylum who had put her in the van after she passed out.

Her gaze got shifted from the faces to the outside. There the Punit was, paying off the inspector in front of her house. And as the van went ahead, she saw Manu frantically running through the shadows on the street, chasing the van named 'St. Mary's Mental Asylum'.

Chapter 19

"Thanks for meeting me here, Nipun," greeted Mugdha as she entered the cafe.

She put down her purse on the corner table and sat down in a chair across Nipun.

Nipun had already ordered a pitcher of coffee for them as he anticipated that the discussion was going to be a long one.

"Tell me everything you know," he said.

"Like I told you before, Sanjana Poddar had called me earlier this week but she was very secretive about everything. She did not give me anything to begin with. She was ranting about her husband coming back from the dead after 10 years. And of course, to me, it sounded obscure, so, I did not take her case. What was weird was when she called, she seemed scared. Now, why would you be scared of a loved one coming back to life?"

"Mysterious woman indeed," Nipun interjected.

"She said something about her son's life in danger after what happened before the night Punit died."

"How did he die?"

"She didn't say."

"Any PM reports or death certificates?"

"Burnt."

"What? What do you mean burnt?"

"Someone destroyed all pieces of evidence of Punit being cremated that day..."

"When was 'that' day?" Nipun questioned.

"She didn't say... just that it was roughly 10 years ago."

"You know what they say, right..." said Nipun leaning back in his chair, "Someone who doesn't tell you the truth..."

"Has more secrets to hide than a liar," completed Mugdha.

She carefully set the opened receipt from the crematorium on the table. It stared at both of them challenging their wits to fit it in the rest of the puzzle.

"She has been admitted to a mental asylum," stated Mugdha looking at the receipt.

"What?"

"I checked with some of the neighbours. They said that a woman was taken away to St. Mary's asylum at 4am."

"St. Mary's?" exclaimed Nipun, "That place is notorious for beating up patients and making them more insane each day."

"Yes, Nipun, I know, which is why we need to find out solid proof to get her out as quickly as possible."

"This seems so entangled and twisted," spat Nipun, "What else did you find out?"

"Nothing..." said Mugdha burying her head in her hands, "Sanjana had strictly told not to investigate invasively such that people know. Apparently, this imposter, as she says has every detail of Punit right."

"How do you mean?"

"His scars, his behaviour, his talking style, his persona, even his knowledge of Sanjana and her son, Manu. It was like he is resurrected back from the dead."

"What about the family? What are they saying about it?"

"Here is where things get super weird. Sanjana's parents have not answered their phones and their whereabouts are unknown. But in her call last night, before the text message, she said that her mother-in-law and her father-in-law reacted like nothing has happened and they deny that there even was a funeral."

The pair looked at the receipt that lay on the table steadily, withholding a malevolent enigma.

"Why would they lie?"

"We need to find out, and soon," declared Mugdha, "The mystery is deeply rooted somewhere in the family. Punit is missing after the capture last night, Manu is missing and Sanjana is in the asylum after allegedly killing their cat."

"It seems like this Punit is pressing the right buttons. I have a theory," said Nipun thoughtfully, holding the receipt in his hands, "There is no doubt that the funeral has taken place for a 35 or 55-year-old Poddar..."

Mugdha hummed, "But what if the said Punit's corpse rolled out before being cremated?"

"Unlikely. The Poddars would have had to pay a lot of people who would have witnessed such an event; also, Sanjana said that she also had gone to the crematorium, right?"

Mugdha nodded.

"So, let's just say that a body was really burnt, it could be either of Punit or of someone else. If it was someone else, why would Punit take 10 years to show up? It seems like a long time, doesn't it?"

Mugdha's eyes narrowed as the picture before her began getting clearer.

"Correct," she gasped, "So it is likely, that the real Punit died that night and someone, who looked like him, took his place years later, researching about Sanjana's family."

"Perhaps a twin..." thought Nipun loudly.

"Not possible, that was my very first guess when I spoke to Sanjana. She and Punit were college sweethearts. Punit was the only son the Poddars had."

"Let me rephrase," corrected Nipun, "A twin that others don't know about."

Mugdha's eyes widened.

"But why would this guy want to hurt a fifteen-year-old kid?" he questioned loudly.

"Sanjana is rich. She had her assets transferred to her son after Punit's untimely death. But he is still a minor and has 3 years to claim everything of his own. Now let's just say that if Sanjana was proven insane, and Manu is still a minor, who gets to handle her businesses?"

"A manager that the district court would appoint..." said Nipun looking intensely at Mugdha.

"Who would most likely, in the absence of Sanjana's parents be..."

"Her son's guardian or father...Punit Poddar," Nipun finished her sentence.

"And if in the interim, Manu were to die," she continued, "Punit would enjoy those rights not just for 3 more years, but for perpetuity."

"Well played, Poddars."

"We need to act fast, before St. Mary's mentally decapitates her."

"Let's meet her now..."

"We can't, visiting hours are in the evening."

"So, let's start with getting to know where this guy works and if there was a twin."

Mugdha called the reception of the office where Sanjana told Punit worked a decade ago before his demise. If according to Sanjana, the new Punit still went to work, the reception would be a perfect place to get in touch with him, pretending she meant business.

The phone rang twice before a lady answered.

"Hello, Congrutech limited... how may I help you?"

"Hi," said Mugdha putting the phone on speaker, "I have some business with your engineers...Mr. Punit Poddar... Could you please transfer the line to him?"

"Just give me a moment, ma'am, I will look for his extension."

The lady put Mugdha's call on hold. After a brief wait that seemed forever, the static was broken by the lady's voice.

"I am sorry, ma'am. Mr Poddar no longer works with us."

"Where does he work then?"

"I do not know, ma'am. Mr Poddar left the company 10 years ago. Hope you have a great day."

And she hung up.

"Mugs, we have to go back to the horror house," stated Nipun, "We need to find out dirt on this shady man."

Mugdha agreed as they both got up and left.

"Let's begin with a birth certificate. We need to pay a visit to the hospital that delivered him to check if a baby went missing."

A worried Punit tossed in a bundle of fresh notes across the desk to a doctor of St. Mary's Mental Asylum.

"Please take care of my wife, she is really sick," said Punit crying.

"We will take care of it, Mr Poddar," said Dr Tania as she took the money.

Punit exited the chamber of the doctor and ran into a familiar face. He looked at him in the eye, smiled, nodded once and crossed him.

Dr Shukla looked back at him, smiled and entered Dr Tania's chamber for an external opinion on the case.

They both entered back into the dark belly of the beast, taking on different rooms to look for documents.

Manu's room was completely turned upside down. Everything was out of the cabinets, so there was nothing hidden that containment.

Mugdha went to Sanjana's bedroom and Nipun went into the drawing-room.

"Mugs, I see a safe here," shouted Nipun from downstairs, "Do you know the code?"

"No…" she shouted back while scanning documents in Sanjana's room.

She tapped every piece of clothing to look for anything that could help when she suddenly felt something.

"Got it!" she gasped, looking at an employee ID card that read- 'Punit Poddar'.

She quickly googled the name of his company and found out the phone number of a head engineer.

'Let's see what your colleague has to say,' she thought while dialling the number.

"Hello," said a man angrily.

"Hi, I am Lekha," pretended Mugdha, "Calling from Indian Engineers awards. This is regarding one of your colleagues, Mr Punit Poddar, who is selected for the final round. He has listed you as a reference."

"The audacity of that man…" grunted the man, *"Madam, I have no idea why you have even selected someone with no credentials. I am his boss. His behaviour is so arbitrary… he randomly goes missing for weeks without informing, doesn't talk to anyone, highly reserved and hasn't shown up for work for God knows how long. And whenever he speaks, he speaks in strange riddles."*

"What do you mean?" asked Mugdha with curiosity ignoring the voices of shifting furniture from downstairs.

"Last time he went missing, he informed a teammate that he had to plan a funeral in advance just like the one he had attended earlier. What do you infer from this? We should never have hired him after we came to know that he did not quit his previous organisation, he absconded. People thought he was dead for a good 8 months… And if you talk to him, madam, tell him to never give my number to anyone like you and that he no longer works here."

And the man hung up.

Mugdha rushed downstairs to update Nipun, but he was not to be found.

"*Nipun…*" she announced.

"Here…come quick," he said in a muffled voice as he emerged from a wall that looked like a dead-end.

Mugdha's eyes widened.

"What's that?" she asked Nipun.

"You have to see to know," he replied, pushing the wall inside into a small room.

The room was shelved with books on psychosis, with Punit's clothes lying on a chair, and in the middle of the room, on the table was a glass beaker and stirrer, beside which lay a packet of a drug called –'Haldol'.

"Oh my God!" said Nipun, "Haldol can cause hallucinations. He is experimenting by mixing it with hydroxy tryptamine on someone to drive them crazy. Wanna bet, I can name his lab rat in 3 guesses?"

Mugdha's body refused to move as she was stuck in a corner holding a book open to a page on induced schizophrenia, staring at a handmade bookmark that said-

'I murdered him the night before the funeral. I died, and now I am reborn.'

Nipun came and stood behind her with his eyebrows pressed together as he slowly flipped the bookmark.

It said- 'I feared the dark until I smiled in the fire that burnt me; now the dark fears me.'

"Pun, for a mentally unstable person, who would know every detail about you and your family, more than you can even remember?"

"The psychiatrist!" Nipun gasped.

Chapter 20

"Stop it…stop," screamed Sanjana as she resisted to walk any further inside the darkness of St Mary's mental asylum.

She was strapped in a straight jacket, escorted by two ward boys and a nurse into the endlessness of the asylum. No one had asked her for any clarification of any question. Her opinion did not matter about the whole incident and the mad hat was pinned on her by default. The plan was not just sinister, but it was chalked with meticulous details. Sanjana wondered how wide the curtains of this showman had spread.

Sanjana was dragged in.

"I am not mad," she shouted at one of the ward boys, "Get your hands off me; I am not mad."

The outburst of Sanjana spread like wildfire in the asylum as the patients all started chanting hellishly and unequivocally,

"I am not mad…I am not mad…I am not mad…"

Sanjana quickly realised that she had made a terrible mistake. The only way to get out of that place was to cooperate as much as she could and pretend that she was completely fine with everything. It also meant no more Punit is an imposter story. She had to get out quickly because her son's life was at stake. Her mind started plotting every next move like a seasoned chess player.

The staff stopped dragging her as she stopped resisting. They waited at a locked, barred gate at the end of the common room passage. There were only two ways to go- left and right. It seemed like the guards were waiting for instructions.

"Now be good," instructed the nurse as they began to leave, "The better you behave, the earlier you will be released."

Sanjana knew exactly what she meant. Assessments happened every day. She just needed to consistently show sanity to the resident doctor for him to sign her release.

Sanjana smiled and nodded in agreement.

The staff left to call the resident doctor leaving Sanjana alone at the end of the common room.

She looked around. She was surrounded by people desperately needed help but seemed abandoned. There was an old man who was in a rocking chair who caught her attention. He was facing the wall, frantically making circles in the air like his life depended on it. Sanjana felt a natural force of attraction towards him as she began walking in his direction.

"Stop." she heard from behind like a warning.

She turned around, and there was this young girl, likely in her teens, staring at her. She walked a little closer and Sanjana walked back.

"Don't worry," said the girl nicely, "I won't hurt you. My name is Dolly," and she extended her hand.

Sanjana refused to take her hand.

"Don't be scared. This is the docile unit. We mean no harm to people. The criminal ward is at the left of the passage. They don't get unsupervised time in the common room," she explained.

Sanjana reluctantly took her hand and dared to ask,

"What- what's wrong with you?"

"Nothing," smiled Dolly, "I am just… just… socially unfit as per my family. But worry not, after 3 months here, this already feels like my family."

Dolly seemed absolutely 'normal' to her. She spoke, behaved and dressed in a way that did not belong to that place.

"Why did you stop me?" Sanjana asked.

Dolly smiled and replied, "He is Dhope Uncle. He used to be a surgeon, but he got sucked into pretty dark stuff before he lost his sanity. His wife was killed before his eyes, and he was made to inscribe a message in blood with his son at gunpoint. He keeps inscribing those symbols in mid-air now refusing to stop. He thinks that the killer will shoot his son."

Sanjana ignored everything she said. To her, more important was to focus on what she was seeing. Her attention was caught by the people standing outside, in the front lawn. She approached the barred window and looked through it carefully.

It was Punit, Manu, her in-laws, her parents and Dr Shukla entangled in what seemed like a very heated argument. She saw Manu standing behind her mother, looking angry. She had not heard from her parents in a long while; it seemed like her genius son had gotten hold of them and told them everything that was happening.

Her father seemed pissed. His face had turned all red and he kept pointing to the doctor and Punit yelling something. It seemed like he was threatening them to let Sanjana go. Manu seemed more sad than angry. He was yelling from behind his grandmother, Ratna, in the chaos looking at his grandpa, telling him something pointing at his dad. Dr Shukla and Arati stood face to face shaking their head from side to side, not trying to participate in the conversation. Punit seemed equally enraged throwing both his hands in the air when Manu's attention was suddenly drawn to his mother standing in the window frame.

The noisy common room suddenly got silent as the doctor marched in with the ward boys and the nurses. They headed for Sanjana straightaway with a tiny petri dish containing some white pills.

"Sanjana Poddar," said the psychiatrist Dr Tania, "How are you?"

She took a notepad, lowered her spectacles and scribbled something on a piece of paper.

"According to your previous doctor, Dr Shukla, you have schizophrenia," announced Dr Tania, "Do you know what that is?"

Sanjana gasped as she knew what was happening.

'What rubbish?' she thought, 'This doctor is compromised too. You think I don't know what schizophrenia is?'

"Yes, ma'am," replied Sanjana faking a pleasant smile, "But why would you say I have it?"

"According to Dr Shukla," said Dr Tania, "You showed signs of hallucination. You imagined things that weren't there."

'That bastard,' thought Sanjana, 'Instead of telling the truth, he sold me out. Whatever happened to doctor-patient confidentiality.'

"May I get an example, ma'am?" asked Sanjana nicely.

"Like you reported that your husband was dead, but he is pretty much alive, didn't you?"

'Oh my God! I think the fake Punit figured out how the real Punit died, Manu has to be protected under any circumstance now.'

"I think," said Sanjana, "There is some misunderstanding. Ask my parents, they can tell you about the funeral."

"No one has to ask anyone anything, Sanjana," said Dr Tania pushing the petri dish close to her mouth, "Your doctor has mentioned everything. If Punit really died, how did he die?"

'Oh no..." she thought, 'They know everything. They know I lied. But how?'

"Sorry, ma'am," Sanjana gulped, "He didn't. I just got confused."

"That's what I thought," said Dr Tania shoving the medicines in her face, "Now be a good girl and swallow the pills. The more you cooperate, the easier for me to let you go."

Sanjana shook her head up and down, forcing a smile, but her eyes had welled up.

"And till you get out, the court decided to transfer your assets to the adult in your immediate family, which is your husband, Punit."

Sanjana placed the pills on her tongue and acted like she had swallowed it.

"Thank your stars, Sanjana," continued Dr Tania, "That we are placing you in the docile ward even after you killed your cat. But if it were up to me..." she leaned in, "I would throw you in the criminal chamber."

Dr Tania left yelling, "Room 31."

"B-Bathroom?" asked Sanjana after being untied, trying not to move the pills under her tongue. She needed to spit them out before they disintegrated in her mouth surrounded by saliva.

A nurse escorted her inside and stood out, guarding the door. Sanjana quickly spat the pills and gargled twenty times before getting out.

The nurse then escorted her to her room. It was empty, like a shell. The 15x15 room only contained two beds about 6 feet apart and a '*Bhagvadgita*' on each bed.

Sanjana looked at the other bed and looked at the nurse.

"This is for your roommate," she said in a condescending tone, "We were instructed to keep you with the most non-threatening person, God knows why. You don't get anything else except this book. Read," she instructed as she bent down and removed Sanjana's *chappals*.

"What are you doing?" asked Sanjana retracting her feet.

The nurse smacked her head with the same *chappal* and said, "We don't keep anything that can be used as a weapon.

Now go out in the common room and come here back with your roommate Dolly when you are told."

Sanjana rushed back to the common room with the TV playing loudly and about 6 patients sitting in front of it and watching. Others were distracted doing their own things; some were just standing and looking into nothingness, some were near the music system increasing and decreeing the volume and others were just sitting on the couch.

Sanjana's eyes got drawn to the window where she saw a face that could always give her hope even in the darkest of the times. It was Manu. She surreptitiously stood near the window, not looking at Manu.

"Mom," whispered Manu, "Don't worry, hang in there. Dad…I mean the fake dad, he seems to have bought everyone. But *Nanu* got very angry. Apparently, at his request, *Nani -Nanu,* had gone somewhere out of town in a village or something till someone told them about you. He was mad when I told him everything the fake dad did. He is trying to find out ways to prove it and has threatened him that if you are not released tonight, he will have to pay very heavily."

"What did Punit say then?" Sanjana whispered, looking away in an empty corner so that no one got suspicious.

"He has somehow paid the entire staff to keep you in check and shove medicines down your throat till you actually go insane. He also made sure that your parents or I don't have visiting rights…"

"He can do that?" huffed Sanjana.

"He can, mom, and he did. Everyone is involved head deep in this."

"Be safe, Manu. It seemed like the doctor knew about how Punit died."

"What?" gasped Manu, "She knows he was killed?"

Sanjana shushed Manu loudly. The nurse looked at her and she smiled nodding.

"I am staying with *nani.* Don't worry, I will be safe. But keep behaving well, they should not get even the slightest scent of what is going on. Okay, mom?"

Sanjana hummed.

"Also, *nanu* is getting you out tonight. I don't know for sure, but most likely he has paid the guy on night duty to secretly get you out, unless dear daddy gets to know."

"I don't understand... Why is he doing this?" questioned Sanjana, "Is this about money?"

"Doesn't seem so," Manu whispered, "I can't put a pin on his plan, but his body language is more vindictive than greedy. Maybe he knows..."

"There is not another soul in this world except the both of us who knows that I killed Punit."

"You did it for me..." Manu interrupted.

"I am not sucking you into this discussion".

"Mom..." warned Manu as he got attentive, "I have to go, someone is coming. But act normal, keep a lookout for tonight. And if grandpa fails, I swear to you that there is not another night that you will spend in this hell hole. I promise I will break you free."

"Be safe, Manu, don't let that imposter hurt you."

"Don't worry, mom," Manu said, running away, "Vengeance will be served."

Chapter 21

"Shouldn't we call the police?" questioned Nipun.

"And say what?" spat Mugdha, "We will have a tough time explaining what we were doing snooping around in the house of horrors when we came across a completely innocent looking chemistry lab shielded from the rest of the house, to let's say, keep their teenage son away from experimenting...

"When you put it that way, it doesn't seem negative at all."

"Besides, remember how Sanjana mentioned about police also being a part of this plan?"

Nipun nodded.

Mugdha quickly took a picture of everything in that room on her phone and saved it to a folder named 'Poddars'. Nipun looked around trying to find more clues but his thoughts were wandering elsewhere.

"Mugs," he called Mugdha, "Why would Sanjana forbid you from speaking to anyone if she has something very dark to hide?"

"I am frustrated too..." agreed Mugdha, "But I would be concerned too if everyone around me seemed to be taking sides with my husband who wants to kill my child."

"Let's split up," suggested Nipun, "You go and find out about this Punit's employment history and in the meanwhile, this funeral receipt has been haunting me for a long time. I know it's a long shot that I will even get something out of this, but my gut says that there is some strange secret burning on those grounds."

"Cool," said Mugdha marching out, taking off her rubber gloves, "You may want to throw those gloves and the mask into the fire too," she joked as they both left.

Nipun entered a few feet into the crematorium and the heat from the flames of a live-fire had already swallowed him in itself. He was still processing his plan as Sanjana had instructed non-invasive sleuthing. How could he get the right answers without asking any questions or raising any suspicion?

He entered a small room that separated the cremation grounds from the office where he found a thin old man, possibly in his late fifties or early sixties, sitting across the counter. His skin was dark, as if it absorbed the harsh reality of death and reflected the grief of the families that came there. He had the most empathetic eyes Nipun had seen, and his clothes were as humble as the rest of him.

"Sir," Nipun cried crocodile tears. He hated himself for doing that to the old guy, "Sir, my family separated after my *dadu's* death. My uncles took away all his belongings and his property. All his pictures, letters, everything is gone," he couldn't believe it was all impromptu, "My father has the onset of Alzheimer's and reminding him of grandpa is the only way to refresh his memory.

I have this receipt," he showed the washed off receipt, "I show this to him, he reads it and his memory goes back by 10 years to the cremation of *dadu* right here. He cries and then suddenly remembers everything. Please, sir, help me. Can you make a new receipt for me?"

The old man took the receipt in his hands and carefully observed it.

"Son, it is illegal to give a receipt like that. I am sorry," he declared in a shaky voice, "I could have renewed it if the print was legible, but I can't really do anything."

"Sir, please," begged Nipun.

"You know, my family has run this crematorium for more than 50 years now. We don't do this for money, we do this for people," he stood up wobbling, picked something in the dustiest corner of the shelf, brushed off an old notebook and opened up a page on his desk, "I see so many deaths every day that I am afraid I don't even remember my father's funeral."

He grabbed a pen and looked at Nipun.

"This is our old receipt book, so it doesn't mean anything, I will write it just for your father, but it is practically useless. After my old man passed away four years ago, we changed the name of the crematorium from 'Matoshri' to 'Sai' in honour of my father. Tell me son what was your *dadu's* name?"

Nipun carefully said 'Sambhaji Inamdar' and gave other details so as it looked close to whatever was legible on the washed-up receipt.

Mugdha entered in Congrutech premise, where Punit worked 10 years ago in the pretext of being a potential business client dealing with whom she thought could be Punit's teammate at that time. As she waited at the reception, she realised there was a biometric barrier for the employees to cross.

"Hi, Miss Sharma, I am Pratik, we spoke on the phone," called a formally dressed middle-aged man.

He welcomed Mugdha in a meeting room and began presenting her his proposal. She faked her interest in his proposal and sat through it with patience. Once he was done, it was time for her Q&A.

"Excellent presentation, Pratik," faked Mugdha, "But we have had a bad experience with your firm in the past. Not receiving phone calls, missing deadlines, lying to your clients, substandard delivery..."

"I am not sure what you mean, Miss Sharma," said Pratik.

"You see, we worked with one of your associates, Mr Punit Poddar about a decade ago and did not have a pleasant experience."

Pratik took some time to remember who Mugdha was talking about.

"Oh, I am surprised," he exclaimed, "He was one of our top-performing tech guys. I am sure there would have been some misunderstanding. Besides, I don't know what he was doing in a sales pitch with you folks. He was a big bold recluse. Good thing he was hired by RGS then," he winked.

That was Mugdha's cue to leave and head to RGS to find out through trails of fieldwork what this Punit was up to.

Nipun met Mugdha in Sunrise cafe around 4:30pm.

"Anything?" he asked.

"Yes, you?" she replied with a question.

"Yes. You go first."

"I went to all the 7 companies he has worked for in the last ten years," she stated, "He did a disappearing act 10 years ago and joined his next company 4 months late..."

"So, it takes 4 months to wake the dead?" joked Nipun.

"But, listen to this," interrupted Mugdha, "His erratic behaviour continued. He was a social recluse- no friends, ate lunch alone, never attended any office parties like he lived in the shadows unnoticed. However, he was consistent, went to work regularly until a year or two back..."

"What happened then?"

"He went missing again... for four months. No calls or anything at work. They declared him absconded. And then the new job, irregular visits and the erratic behaviour continued. And guess what..."

"What?"

"When his old colleague asked him about his disappearing acts, he said Punit said it with a creepy smile, that one funeral in the past had changed his entire life, now he is spending time in planning another one just like the old one."

"Such creepy vibes, Mugs."

"Okay, now you go," she permitted.

"So," began Nipun, "I am now certain that there indeed was a funeral, no doubt about that. But what struck me was, the old guy said that they rebranded the entire crematorium about four years back."

Mugdha's eyes narrowed as she slowly felt a chill crawling up her spine.

"This is the new receipt," he continued, keeping the old one and the new one side by side, "So, either someone took the efforts to renew it, or the funeral took place not before 4 years ago."

Mugdha inhaled loudly, but before she could speak, Nipun asked, "Did you go to Sanjana's workplace?"

Mugdha hummed in agreement.

"One company," she answered, "Most of the time she took work from home, loner, private life, and a good performer, nothing much to report about her."

"Then let's go to Manu's school."

"Home-schooled."

"What the..." sighed Nipun, "This entire family is such a big enigma. What if the reality is nothing around the three of them? What if the bigger agenda is something else..." he paused thinking more with his conspiracy theory side of the brain, "What if Punit's death, Sanjana going to the Asylum and Manu being in danger are irrelevant?"

"I sincerely hope that you are wrong," gulped Mugdha covered in chills, "I must meet Mrs Poddar right away. All our questions will be answered if we come to know who died that night."

Chapter 22

'I need to cooperate the best I can so that there is no reason they won't let me out tonight,' thought Sanjana as she sat on the couch in the common room near Dolly, her new roomie.

The patients were all dressed in the asylum gowns- pink for females, blue for males and green for the one who needed critical attention. Sanjana fell under the last category due to her concussion which as per the hospital was caused because she slipped and fell.

The walls were poorly patched with exposed wires. The television was as old as the film being played on it. The window curtains were dusty, holding a variety of infections. The floor smelled of phenyl but still seemed like it needed a desperate cleaning. The entire chaos was 'maddening', thought Sanjana, 'How can someone even expect to get better in such a place?'

"What's to the left, beyond those bars?" asked Sanjana to Dolly.

"That's the criminally insane ward," she replied, "People who are deemed dangerous by the society or court are admitted there."

"So, the bars are to keep them in?"

"More like to keep us out…" she said looking at the prison gate, "A 'Ward A' patient had once gone in by mistake and he got beaten to within an inch of his life."

Sanjana gulped.

"It's really sad. The life of those inside that ward. We are still better here. They get to come out only once for a couple of hours in the morning, that too only to mop the floors, cut the grass and clean the toilets," she pointed at a middle-aged hefty ward boy, "You see that guy? I have even heard he rapes and abuses the females inside..."

"Oh my God!" exclaimed Sanjana, "And no one complains?"

"Well, a criminal psycho accusing a noble married worker of rape? Who will you believe?"

A gentle tear rolled out of Sanjana's eye.

"I sincerely hope, sister," said Dolly placing a hand on her shoulder, "That you get out of here soon. Else, this will make you crazy."

She realised that Sanjana was shivering.

"Here is what you will do," continued Dolly, "The doctor comes on rounds twice a day, mornings and evenings after visiting hours. It is a regular examination with a checklist. She will ask you some stupid questions and based on your response, she will determine if you are insane or not."

"What-What if I remain silent?" asked Sanjana.

"Boom... declared clinically insane."

Sanjana looked at dolly with horror.

"Listen carefully... There will be some objective questions like is your stomach upset? Answer as normally as you can. Don't just say yes or no, elaborate only a little, like my stomach was upset this morning, but I am much better now. Although, I am more concerned about the open-ended questions. That is the true test. Like vultures, these guys wait for you to use one wrong word and snap..." she snapped, "you are booked."

Dolly's advice was interrupted by a deafening alarm that exploded across the room. The already chaotic place burst into an uproar of entropy dancing and jumping all around the place. The handful staff of 4 tried to contain the fifty-odd patients in the common room.

"What's happening?" asked Sanjana.

"Visiting hours," said Dolly.

In the mayhem, a nurse escorted Sanjana outside in the meeting area. Sanjana had a visitor. The nurse sat her in front of a young female.

"Mugdha," said Mugdha, who had come in a heavy disguise meeting Sanjana for the first time, "We had spoken on the phone earlier."

Sanjana sat uncomfortably in her chair, pressing her patient gown between her knees, feeling exposed. She avoided eye contact and voiced,

"I had hoped we would meet under better circumstances."

"Don't worry, ma'am," said Mugdha compassionately, "I will get you out of here soon, I promise."

Sanjana leaned into her and said, "My dad is getting me out of here tonight, he has an arrangement. If my imposter husband doesn't meddle, I will not spend a night here."

"As instructed by you, I haven't met or contacted any of your family or friends to avoid any suspicion. I have been very inconspicuous about everything. But I must say, ma'am, I have very bad news."

Sanjana felt like the universe was plotting against her.

"There are no records of Punit dying. So, our best is that he was alive this whole time."

"What? How are you so sure?"

"He has worked on and off all these 10 years. He has strong alibis. Did you know of the room inside the rear wall in your house?"

"What? No… what is in it?"

"It looked like Punit's den, he has books on psychiatry, and it looked like he was experimenting with some drugs… one of them being Haldol."

"What? That's my medicine…"

"Haldol is a prescription drug, ma'am, who gave it to you?"

"Well, my psychiatrist, Dr Shukla, of course.'

"Don't you find it fishy that he consulted on your case here? Did he drop any truth bombs that he had never told you?"

Sanjana thought and replied with eager eyes,

"Not him, but the resident here told me that he told her I have schizophrenia."

"Snitch..." said Mugdha, "He needs a proper visit from me now."

"No..." snapped Sanjana, "Why don't you focus on proving that Punit died?"

"But, ma'am, I just told you. There is no solid evidence of his death. It is very likely that he was alive the whole time."

"But...the funeral," teared Sanjana.

"Yes... there was a funeral, we checked. But it was not Punit who died."

"But...that's impossible. Punit died that night. We saw... we checked many times. I did it myself..."

"What was that now?"

Sanjana gulped, pulling her hair back.

"You promise me, promise me to get me out of here. My Manu, he is not safe out there," she cried, "You need to look out for him while I am here. Please... He is not safe..."

Sanjana had finally broken down. The imposter had managed to break her bones and her spirit. The only true light left in her life, her son, seemed to be dimming.

"I will..." responded Mugdha, "Not unless you tell me what happened that night."

Sanjana tried to be strong, but the river in her eyes seemed perennial. Clenched eyebrows, shivering body, and in breathless whispers she replied in a feeble voice.

"I loved Punit, more than life. But after Manu was born, things changed between us. He was changed. Like something evil in him had awoken. He hit my little boy, yelled at him, even threatened him. Manu was conditioned to be a fragile child, not because he was fragile, but because his father was the embodiment of the devil, so dominant and negative. He once chased away poor Manu like hell itself was after my son. That night, things got too heated, I heard him whispering to himself that he is going to beat Manu to a pulp.

I couldn't just stare at the abuse. I knew Punit was taking Cyclosporin for his blood pressure. I just mixed some of it in a Chinese herbal tea. Did you know, herbal tea causes accelerated heart rate as a cardiovascular exercise? That's how you simulate cardio weight loss with all such teas..."

Mugdha listened to every word without realising that the shiver in Sanjana's body was reflecting in Mugdha's legs too.

"After he drank his tea," continued Sanjana, "He went to Manu's room, getting angry at something. It was not always like this, you know?" Sanjana forced a sad smile, "Just that Punit had so many expectations that Manu just wasn't able to live up to them."

"What happened next?" asked Mugdha.

"He started strangling Manu in his bed... I ran upstairs and found him choking his own son just because he was allergic to some food and wouldn't eat it.

I quickly broke the pair and asked Punit to take his blood pressure medicine, so that he would feel better. And guess what?"

"He overdosed," completed Mugdha, "And died of an induced heart attack that seemed perfectly natural."

Sanjana nodded.

"I just meant for him to pass out, but the tea and the medicines raced his heart too much. I was just looking out for my son."

Mugdha didn't realise that she had teared up too. Her hands were as cold as Sanjana's when she took them.

"Punit's mother, Arati, is a doctor too. She checked his pulse, and he had indeed passed."

"It could be possible that he was still alive then," said Mugdha, "And the mother and son plotted this whole thing."

"Maa would never do that," spat Sanjana, "I love her more than I love my own mother. And she loved Manu the most."

"You said she denied of any funeral when she came to your house?"

Sanjana nodded.

"There," said Mugdha, "There is your speck of doubt…"

Sanjana began constantly wiping her tears, shaking her head side to side, cursing what was going on in her life. She felt guilty for not being there for Manu when he needed her the most.

"You know," said Sanjana in a broken whisper, "I loved Punit sincerely. After he passed, every day I wanted him to come back. And now that he did, I pray every day that he would go away."

"Ma'am," asked Mugdha, "Is there anyone else in this entire picture, someone who can perhaps take a stand for you and Manu. A testimony from an important non-related person can really help to get you out, in case tonight doesn't go as planned."

"There is Manu's tuition teacher. He is the best in town. Dr Kartik Ahluwalia, he is a professor of mathematics and physics in the Guru Nanak University. He was with us for some time. Especially when Punit was not in the house and when he suddenly appeared."

Mugdha took a mental note of the name and gave Sanjana a reassuring hug before leaving. She took the details of where Punit was born to cross-check the twin theory.

The alarm exploded again. It was time for Sanjana to meet her doctor and prove that she was not insane.

Mugdha went out and called Nipun immediately. She told him everything that she had learnt from her visit. Their theory was wrong. It seemed like a detailed plot of vengeance.

"Wait a sec..." interrupted Nipun, "What did you say? Kartik Ahluwalia?"

"Yes," agreed Mugdha, "Professor in University."

There was a prolonged silence on the phone when Nipun broke it,

"Check your chat... I have sent you a picture."

Mugdha opened the picture. It was a recent newspaper article. She gasped loudly as she read-

"Local genius Dr Kartik Ahluwalia commits suicide in the classroom."

Chapter 23

"How are you feeling, Sanjana?" asked Dr Tania.

"Slightly afraid of the change in environment," answered Sanjana confidently, "But besides that, I am fine."

Dr Tania secretly wrote something on her notepad. 'Maybe I overdid it,' thought Sanjana.

"What about this environment scares you?"

'Keep it cool, Sanju… Answer as casually as possible. Your release is planned tonight.'

"Well," inhaled Sanjana forcing a smile, "Would you rather live here than your house?"

The pen moved vehemently.

"Does your head hurt?"

"It hurt in the morning, but I am fine now."

"What about your hallucinations? Do you still think your husband is dead?"

'Yes… pretty much,' she thought.

"It seems like a nightmare now," said Sanjana, choosing her words very carefully, "Losing him was the worst feeling I ever had and when I woke up, and he was back, I did not know my dreams from my reality. But I know now. I wronged my Punit so much."

She began crying fake tears.

The doctor glared at her through her spectacles intensely.

"How was your married life like?"

"Is…" corrected Sanjana smartly, "We are just like any other couple. Punit is a strict father and I am a lenient mother.

We have differences in our methods to raise our child, but which couple doesn't?"

"And how well does your boy adjust to these differences? Abhimanyu, right?"

"Children always have a problem when their parents fight. But Punit and I always made sure that Manu never had to watch us fight. He is being raised as a kid full of love and compassion."

'Love and compassion...' thought Sanjana as the voice in her head scoffed, 'I am scared for my boy's life and this woman is clearly bought and is now faking her interest in my life.'

"Do I sense anxiety when you speak about your son and Mr Poddar in the same sentence?"

Sanjana controlled her rapid breathing so that it made no audible sound. Had the doctor noticed her anxiety?

"It's just that this place and the whole interrogation is so intimidating. It makes me nervous."

Sanjana was sweating profusely now.

"Have you noticed at times that your body does not move? Like it freezes in one place and doesn't react."

Flashes of Punit entering the door and Sanjana freezing in the same place flooded her memory.

Drops of perspiration trickled down her forehead.

"No," she lied.

"One-word response… interesting."

Sanjana's lips parted to help her fill her lungs adequately. She was feeling breathless.

"Have you ever hurt someone intentionally?"

Her brain projected the image of her in the kitchen wearing rubber gloves, wiping off the cat blood from the bowls.

Her feet began shaking involuntarily.

"No," she lied again trying to speak more than a syllable, but words refused to come out.

"Have you ever heard voices that you couldn't explain?"

Sanjana shook her head side to side, looking down at her bare shivering feet feeling dizzy and out of breath. She felt like she was choking and about to throw up at the same time.

"And what about Punit… did you kill him?"

Sanjana collapsed on the floor with an anxiety attack reaching out to Dr Tania to grab her hand. Her eyes were shut as she saw the doctor refusing to give her a hand for help. And the last thing she saw before losing consciousness was a pair of ward boys running towards her.

"Wake up," Sanjana heard a sharp commanding whisper.

"Wake up!" she heard it again.

Her eyes opened to a cemented ceiling with water seepage patches and cobwebs in the corner.

"Wh-What happened?" asked Sanjana to Dolly, feeling disoriented.

"That bitch triggered an anxiety attack in you," said Dolly.

Sanjana got up and looked outside the window. It was pitch black.

"What time is it?" she asked.

"It's late," said Dolly from her side of the bed, "You have been out for a long time. They put you here."

"No…no…no…no," said Sanjana trying to get up from the bed.

"What's the matter?" asked Dolly getting out of her bed as well.

Sanjana began moving toward the door still feeling disoriented.

"My son told me to keep a lookout for tonight. My dad had the papers of my release."

Dolly jumped in front of the door blocking Sanjana's way.

"What release?" she asked.

"I am supposed to be released tonight," said Sanjana taking one step forward.

But Dolly placed a hand on her chest and pushed her back gently. Sanjana fumbled a few steps back sitting on the bed.

"And what about me?" She cocked her head, innocently, "You will leave your best friend here?"

"I will come back for you," said Sanjana getting up.

"He said that too," said Dolly moving towards Sanjana. Her eyes screamed of evil and her voice, demonic, "He never came back for me."

"But I will," said Sanjana leaning backwards in her bed as Dolly approached closer.

"Oh no, you won't," exclaimed Dolly in blurt of terror as she pinned Sanjana down and sat on her chest. She held both her arms against the bedposts and leaned in.

"Help…" Sanjana tried to scream, but it came out as a broken whisper.

"Say that again," demanded Dolly.

Tears trickled down Sanjana's eyes as she desperately tried to get out of Dolly's strong grip.

"Say that again!" commanded Dolly, "Loudly this time."

"H-Help…Help!"

Her screams generated other screams across the hallway. Patients from multiple rooms started to scream for help, like it was a daily routine.

Dolly slapped Sanjana.

"You know why I am here?" whispered Dolly, "They say I have bipolar disorder…that I can't control my anger. But you know what…"

"Pl-Please…please," begged Sanjana crying among the random screams.

Dolly released her grip from Sanjana's wrists and brought that tight grip on Sanjana's neck. She pressed her windpipe, taking pleasure in choking her.

"You know what," she continued as Sanjana struggled for breath under her, slowly turning red, "I was completely aware of what I was doing when I slit my mother's throat."

Sanjana flailed her hands in random directions, eyes popping out, and the veins on her forehead ready to burst.

"That bitch was going to abandon me," she said innocently, "You know, just like you, you bitch."

Dolly put her back into choking Sanjana even more.

"And don't act so innocent, I know you killed your husband. I heard you talking to your visitor friend."

Sanjana's hands struggled to release the grip or to hurt dolly in any way. She was losing her strength when her right hand suddenly felt the hard rim of the *bhagvadgita* lying on her bed.

She grabbed the book tightly in her hand and hit Dolly right between her eyes with all the energy she had left in her.

Dolly's hands retracted in response. Sanjana delivered three more blows with the thick rim and the sharp edge of the book to cause dolly to lose her guard. Sanjana pushed her off her chest, making her fall on the floor. She grabbed the book tightly, ran out of the door and latched it behind her.

Sanjana sprinted to the end of the locked passage, watching the dark passage of the criminal ward guarded by a prison-like gate. She knew she had to take a sharp left at the intersection leading her to the common room. She could wait there till someone comes to take her home.

She was worried about Manu as she knew that Punit was going to take revenge. He was coming for Manu. And the only person Manu trusted was his mother.

Sanjana took a sharp left into the common room and froze at the sight of what she could not believe was true. She pinched herself many times to confirm that it wasn't a dream or a hallucination.

There she was, another imposter, near the exit door, leaving the horrors of the asylum. She looked exactly like Sanjana, wore the same clothes Sanjana was wearing when she came in.

As the door opened, Sanjana saw her dad's car parked outside as a ward boy escorted her out secretly.

Sanjana tried to scream, but Dolly had choked her so badly that her scream was almost the whisper.

The woman looked behind, saw Sanjana through the glass that parted the patient and the visitor area; she smiled at her, waved, and then shut the exit door behind her.

Sanjana heard her father's car drive away.

Chapter 24

"I found Punit's birth certificate, Mugs," said Nipun after checking in the safe of the Poddar residence, "The doctor that delivered him has retired now."

"And?" asked Mugdha, pressing the phone to her ear anxiously sitting on the edge of the backseat of a taxi.

"I met her and after a long conversation, casually started talking about Punit as my school friend and how two girls were mad for him and always wished they were twins... Well, the bottom line is, she confirmed that Punit has no twin sibling."

"Why would she even remember that information?" questioned Mugdha, "It was so long back, and I am pretty sure she would have delivered many babies in her career."

"Here is where things got interesting..." interrupted Nipun, "Dr Arati Poddar, Punit's mother is her very close friend and a colleague."

"Doctor?" exclaimed Mugdha.

"Not just any doctor," paused Nipun, "A clinical psychologist."

Mugdha hummed.

"Here is what I think happened," envisioned Nipun, "Sanjana induced a heart attack in Punit to save Manu. After Punit collapsed, she thought he was dead. When Arati arrived and checked Punit's pulse, he was still alive. He would have pretended to be dead and told his mother to declare his death to Sanjana. I mean... there was no one else in the funeral except family. So, it would have been so easy to fool them.

While Sanjana grieved and the guys carried Punit's body outside, Sanjana said that her father had momentarily come to check on her, right? And then Sanjana was stopped from going to the crematorium. The window of opportunity opened for a moment. In that moment, with the assistance of his father and a few goons from the crematorium, Punit would have rolled off and replaced the body with a dummy. And when Sanjana's father arrived, followed by her and Manu, it wasn't real Punit anymore."

Mugdha listened to Nipun intently before speaking,

"I don't know, Nipun. The entire plan can't be based on the assumption that Sanjana's dad would leave the corpse alone. And besides, it was Sanjana's own mother who stopped her from going to the crematorium. In fact, Arati was the one who told her that it was okay to go."

"Don't you see?" interrupted Nipun, "It looks like a perfect crime. No one will blame the innocent mother who insisted on her daughter-in-law going to the crematorium; all the more reason for Sanjana to believe that Punit was dead while they plotted their revenge. Revenge is a big motive, isn't it?"

"It is... but why wait for 10 years?" questioned Mugdha.

"Remember the prescription of Haldol that we found in the secret room in their house?" asked Nipun, "Who do you think has access and knowledge of psychotic drugs? Not an engineer for sure. High doses of psychotic drugs can induce serious psychosis even in a sane human being."

"So, you mean," calculated Mugdha still not completely convinced with her associate's theory, "The decade wait to condition her to a drug that was already prescribed to her by her psychiatrist?"

"Correction," spat Nipun, "It's not Haldol, it's what Punit was attaching it with, another balancing psychotic drug. A decade of anxiety, hallucinations, and an unstable mind, she was already on the edge of sanity..."

"And when he showed himself finally," added Mugdha, "It just tipped her over."

"Exactly," said Nipun, "And poor Kartik Ahluwalia became collateral damage in this plot of revenge."

Mugdha took a long pause before speaking again.

"But what about the funeral receipt not being a decade old? You said it was not older than four years, right?"

"That is the part that is eating me up... that piece, the only piece of evidence that we have, doesn't fit in the larger puzzle at all."

"Meet me outside Dr Shukla's office, it is time we visited this old man," suggested Mugdha

"Do you also think he is involved?" asked Nipun.

"Oh, I know he is," finished Mugdha.

Nipun met Mugdha near Dr Shukla's facility.

"What's our back story?" he asked.

"Same old newlywed couple problems," suggested Mugdha as they went upstairs.

They stood in front of the reception in the waiting area, which was populated with only 2 other people. The neatly dressed receptionist had her register closed in front of her, with a phone playing a video on top of it.

Nipun stood there with Mugdha and cleared his throat loudly.

"Walk-in appointment," he declared.

The receptionist looked at the couple and stood up to face them with a pleasant smile.

"Sorry, sir," she said, "We don't have any slots for walk-in's... but I can give you the next available appointment."

"Perfect," said Mugdha, "When is it?"

"A week later."

All their hopes shattered in that single sentence. In a week, the sun would have set on Sanjana's life forever.

"That's too late," said Nipun, "Please...Please get us something early, it is urgent. You don't even have anyone waiting."

"Sir, the consultation sessions happen in the morning downstairs, done by Dr George, Dr Shukla's apprentice. Therapy sessions by Dr Shukla happen now, each session takes 45 minutes. One is already in, the next 2 are sitting here and the one later just confirmed that he is on his way. I am sorry, I can't help you. Shall I book for next week?"

Nipun seemed visibly annoyed. Mugdha grabbed Nipun to the side, near a water cooler, to discuss the plan so that he did not get them kicked out.

As she took him to the corner, away from the reception, Dr Shukla's office door opened and out came Punit Poddar. He marched to the reception, paid, collected a token and left without turning back.

The receptionist opened the register to strike off his name and Nipun jumped at the opportunity. Before she could close the register again, he jumped in front of her and said aggressively,

"I can't believe you gave an appointment to my friend but not to us," he pointed at Punit who had just entered the lift.

"Excuse me?" said the receptionist feeling offended.

Nipun smartly peeped into her register and read the name she had just stricken off.

"I can't believe Rahul comes to this mediocre place... I am going to give this facility a very negative review."

"Sir," said the receptionist calmly taking Nipun's bait, "Your friend, Mr Rathod, is regular here. It was his twenty-first session, so I am sure he doesn't think our facility is mediocre. He takes the appointment a week in advance, so I insist that you should follow our rules or look for a facility elsewhere."

Nipun slowly walked towards Mugdha and collected her on his way towards the exit.

"Who the hell is Rahul Rathod?" exclaimed Mugdha.

They paused in front of Dr Shukla's office and looked at his locked door.

"There is only one way to find out," finished Nipun.

Chapter 25

The dark circles around her eyes and the redness in them made it obvious that she had not slept a wink that night. She had survived the night clutching the *bhagvadgita* close to her chest to literally use it as a weapon if Dolly were to attack her again. Her cries for help were meaningless to the understaffed asylum because of her 'schizophrenia' tag. No one believed that a docile patient like Dolly would even try to hurt her. They termed it as another one of her hallucinations, and the bruise marks around her neck as self-inflicted. If anything, it just convinced them that she was indeed crazy and should never be let out.

The common room was no different that day than the rest of the days, a complete recipe for turning the sane insane, chaotic and disturbing. Sanjana had spent hours on the couch with her eyes wide open thinking of the other woman released the night before. She knew that her family would stop trying to get her out if they were convinced that the other woman was indeed Sanjana. Where were these duplicates coming from?

"Psst," heard Sanjana from the window. She immediately knew who it was.

She walked straight towards the window and saw Manu standing outside. He had bruises all over his face and a gentle cut on the lip.

"Oh my god!" exclaimed Sanjana in horror, "Who did this, beta?"

"Mom," replied Manu in a whisper, "Don't look here or they will know, please."

Sanjana quickly turned away with her side facing the window and demanded,

"Manu, tell me, who did this?"

"I knew it," inhaled Manu, "Mom, last night, grandpa got you out from here. Or at least we thought it was you. But I knew that there was something not quite right about that woman. When grandma and grandpa went to bed, I went to her room and asked her to make me my favourite juice. Now if it were you or grandma, you'd make me..."

"Beetroot juice, no sugar," finished Sanjana, "and nothing else."

"Exactly," continued Manu, "And she asked me what juice I would like. My doubts confirmed right at that moment and I asked her who she was. So, she pinned me down and beat me and threatened to kill me if I disobeyed."

"That bitch did that?" grunted Sanjana with rage, "I will..."

"Mom," interrupted Manu, "I don't have time. You must get out. Grandma and grandpa won't listen to me if I tell them. They'd think I am crazy too. There are a lot of people involved in this mess, mom. I don't think it is safe."

"What do we do?"

"Not we, you," said Manu, "Now it is all up to you. If they even realise that I am here, they will make it impossible for you to escape."

"Escape?" gulped Sanjana.

"Yes, mom. Tonight, you are breaking out of this hell hole. Now listen to me very carefully..."

Manu pointed at the TV and continued-

"Look at that, loose and exposed wires behind the TV. The electric circuit system is exposed on the ceiling too. You know how to short circuit, don't you?"

Sanjana nodded in agreement.

"Excellent. But the fire will be minuscule in the beginning; it must go unnoticed till it spreads. Can you do anything to spread it quickly?"

"They have hand sanitizers for us everywhere; I will spill a few bottles on the carpet and the curtain. The constant smell of phenyl here would help it go unnoticed and if you remember your class seventh science textbook, hand sanitizers are flammable."

"Perfect," said Manu, feeling proud of his mother who had still managed to keep her sanity in that asylum, "The facility is already understaffed. Do it at night so that the staff number goes down further. The fire will create chaos and all the patients will start panicking. Here is where you plan to escape.

Spend the entire day, behaving as obediently as possible. Gain the trust of the staff. When you start the fire, move away from it so that no one sees you. In that chaos, offer to help the staff members by carrying a few patients outside. This is when they will trust you with the exit unattended."

"Yes," whispered Sanjana, "But what after that? The compound wall will be a big issue and the fire won't reach there."

"You take advantage of being unattended. There is a big hole at the back of the compound wall. This is where I have been coming from. It opens into a thin forest that is connected to the main road. You can come at grandpa's directly and I will meet you there."

"Don't worry, beta. You stay safe. I will take care of this tonight."

"And mom," said Manu in a hurry while looking around, "Do not speak of this with any soul. We don't know who is involved in this. And beware that they will try to prove you insane, make you believe that you belong here so that their cover doesn't blow. Don't take any medicines they give, silently agree to whatever they say. Be smart about it."

Manu shared a last glance with his mother and ran away to the back of the asylum.

Sanjana was mentally preparing for the plan when the common room alarm went off. It was time for them to meet their doctor.

Sanjana went inside Dr Tania's cabin and sat across her on a stainless-steel stool.

After her physical examination, Sanjana began responding to the regular torturous questions of the psychiatrist.

"Sanjana, do you want to talk to your husband?" said Dr Tania out of the blue.

Without waiting for Sanjana to respond, she dialled Punit's number on her phone and gave the phone to Sanjana. The thoughts, of what Manu had told her about gaining their confidence for the escape that night, were running like a giant wheel through her brain.

"Hello," said Punit on the phone and Sanjana's heart sank.

For the first time, she knew it was Punit and not an imposter. He sounded scared on the phone, helpless.

"Sanju," his voice cracked, "Sanju, you need to cooperate with these people. Please tell them whatever they want, or else they will not let me get back to you."

Sanjana knew it was Punit. She could tell with 100 per cent certainty that it was indeed her real husband. But before she could talk to him, Dr Tania snatched her phone away and ended the call.

She looked at Sanjana, piercing her gaze and asked,

"Who was that?"

"P-P-Punit," stammered Sanjana slightly confused.

"And who is that?" she pointed at the Punit sitting outside in the visitor area.

There was the imposter, but what did the real Punit want her to tell the doctor?

"P-P..." Sanjana stuttered.

"It is important that you tell us the truth, my dear," said the doctor.

"An imposter," scoffed Sanjana.

Dr Tania smiled and passed a paper to the nurse accompanying Sanjana.

"Have you heard of Capgras delusion?" asked Dr Tania.

Sanjana shook her head side to side to say no.

"It is also known as the imposter syndrome, where a person suffering from it thinks that a loved one is replaced by an imposter. Someone close to you, like your husband, or a pet or sometimes even yourself. So, tell me Sanjana..."

She leaned in.

"Tell me how you think Punit and Poe were replaced by similar-looking strangers. Or better... tell me if you saw someone as your imposter."

Sanjana could feel her heart in her mouth. Was this another method of inducing an anxiety attack in her or was it really the truth?

'How would she know that I saw my doppelganger last night?' thought Sanjana.

Her breathing had begun to pace, but Manu's bruised face was motivation enough for her to get out and fight for her son's life. And if, the real Punit was somewhere, in captive, save him too.

Sanjana chose to stay silent and not answer the doctor. She had to pretend to be obedient.

The nurse came in again with a few pills in a petri dish.

"How are your hallucinations?" asked Dr Tania, "Seeing someone we don't see?"

"No, ma'am," said Sanjana.

"Really? The nurses told me how they saw you facing away from the window and talking into empty space."

'Thank God they did not see Manu,' thought Sanjana.

"I was singing, ma'am."

"Fair enough," said Dr Tania presenting the petri dish in front of her and signalling her to swallow the pills.

"Sanjana," she continued, "I read your patient history with Dr Shukla. Let me tell you how your nightmares were manifested. You actually see the things first and then imagine them in your dreams."

Sanjana was confused.

"Let me explain," said the doctor, "The sticks and stones in the bathtub, the trail of water, the ripped piece of fabric, all of these appear to you in real life, and then your imagination takes over in the nightmares. It is not uncommon with schizophrenics to go through this. Your sense of reality has distorted, darling. So be a good girl, take these pills and let us help you."

Sanjana took the pills with shaking hands and popped them in her mouth at once. The nurse ensured that she swallowed all the pills before escorting her out of the doctor's cabin to the visiting area where Punit was waiting for her.

Sanjana no longer knew if this really was Punit or an imposter or a figment of her imagination.

She sat across him with moist eyes blurring her vision.

"How are you?" he asked in a sad tone.

Sanjana tried but couldn't gather herself to believe that it was really Punit. Her heart screamed that it was not. He was an imposter and she could not convince her heart otherwise.

"Please," she began crying, "Please, whoever you are, I will do anything you want. If there is God, I will do anything for Him to get back my family. You want money, take the money," she began sobbing, "You want the house, just take it... anything. But give me back my Manu and my real Punit. We will disappear and go somewhere no one knows us. You can have our life. But please..."

Punit's tears rolled from his eyes and fell on the table as he got up without saying anything, leaving an out of breath Sanjana crying desperately in her chair.

Punit came out of the asylum into the compound, wiped off his tears and removed his phone from his pocket. He smiled at the screen and texted-

'We have just reached stage 3, prepare for stage 4.'

Sanjana ran inside a bathroom stall after Punit left. She squatted down in front of the toilet and lodged two fingers down her throat. She gagged and the vomit that projectiled ejected the pills that she had swallowed.

She came out of the stall and stood in front of the bathroom mirror. She had never looked so dreadful in life, red eyes, dark circles, drops of sweat all over her face, and her hair entangled within itself.

She splashed some water on her face, looked into the eyes of her reflection and vocalised,

"There is no force in this world that will stop me from protecting my son. Brace yourself, dear husband, there is a storm coming your way tonight. And even the dimmest corners in hell will not be able to hide you."

Chapter 26

"Mugs," said Nipun coming out of Dr Shukla's facility. He was scrolling through his phone constantly as they crossed the street in the evening city lights. Suddenly he stopped and flashed the phone screen in Mugdha's face, "Remember, the gynaecologist who delivered Punit?"

Mugdha saw the phone screen with a woman's picture on it. She read the caption below- "Doctor Geeta Rathod."

"I thought that it can't be a coincidence that the surnames of the now Punit and of this doctor are the same. So...", he scrolled through his phone further and then flashed the screen back at Mugdha.

The photo of Geeta with two young children bore the caption that read-

'Doctor Geeta with her children Rahul and Disha.'

Nipun grabbed the phone again and flashed another fact.

"Look at that, Mugs. Rahul Rathod died in a car crash about 10 years ago."

Mugdha's body was suddenly covered in chills.

"Do you think that Punit knew about it? About Rahul's death," asked Mugdha.

"If not Punit," said Nipun, "Then Arati definitely knew about Rahul's death. From the way Dr Geeta spoke about Arati, it seemed like they were very close. I am sure that Arati would have gone to console her friend."

"You don't think that his body was the one burnt at the crematorium that day, do you?"

"I am inclined towards believing that," said Nipun.

"So, let's follow your theory," said Mugdha, "Instead of Punit's body being replaced at the crematorium, it was actually Rahul's cremation staged as Punit's cremation. Sanjana witnesses Rahul's cremation and thinks it is of Punit. Punit, in the meantime, plots revenge and shows up in front of Sanjana when she is the most vulnerable."

"Yes," said Nipun, "But the receipt from the crematorium still doesn't fit. I still have so many questions left to answer."

Mugdha knew Sanjana had warned about not directly asking anyone involved in this investigation. She was frustrated that Sanjana herself had given very little to no details of what exactly was going on. It seemed like she and Nipun were constantly coming up with theories but were hitting a dead-end eventually because of lack of evidence.

"Pun," said Mugdha, "I am sick of just sitting around and hypothesising."

She pointed at Dr Shukla's building and suggested, "There are a lot of secrets that man is holding right there in that building. I have a strong feeling that he holds the last piece of the puzzle to the big picture."

She sighed loudly shifting her gaze from the building to Nipun and said,

"It is time we put our Nancy Drew and Sherlock Holmes together and break into his office tonight."

"You stole the words from my mouth, Drew."

Dr Shukla's office was on the second floor of a big corporate building guarded by two security guards. Dr Shukla had rented the entire floor for his work. The reception was right across the lift, and Dr Shukla's big cabin was to the right. His working hours would end at 8pm and the whole office would be shut by 9pm.

The pair knew that it would be difficult to get into the building after his office shut. So, they made up a salon appointment on the third floor so that they could already be in the building.

To get to Dr Shukla's cabin, they had to cross two hurdles- the locked grilled door and then his cabin door. The former was much harder than the latter. The first lock was a heavy metallic one.

"How are we going to open this?" whispered Nipun in the darkness of the second floor.

"Remember what I told you during the Shyamlal case?" said Mugdha sounding pompous, "That..."

"No door is closed," finished Nipun.

Mugdha retrieved a long bobby pin that she stole from the salon on the third floor. She had taught herself how to pick a lock at a very young age. After obsessing about Nancy Drew books, she wanted to be just like her. Have all her skills, be truthful and help people. In a swift movement of her wrists, she picked the thick lock in under thirty minutes. But that wasn't the problem. The problem was to lock it again so that no one in the morning knew that the place had been broken in. Nipun was still figuring out that part.

Mugdha opened the second lock in no time with her bobby pin and a credit card. And the pair was in. Time was of the essence, so they started looking around immediately.

Nipun carefully played with the power switches to light the room enough that they could find what they wanted, but no one from the out would see visible light from the office.

After looking around for some time, Mugdha unlocked the drawers and hit the jackpot.

"Nipun, it's all here."

Nipun's heart skipped a beat. All their efforts were going to come in a conclusive end that night.

In the stack of journals, Mugdha retrieved two most interesting ones; one bearing the name 'Sanjana Poddar' and the other of 'Rahul Rathod'.

She tossed Sanjana's journal to Nipun who sat on Dr Shukla's desk and started reading every page of it from the beginning.

Mugdha, on the other hand, sat on the floor, reading Rahul's journal under the lamplight.

"Looks like he is not very talkative," said Mugdha looking at the almost blank pages from the journal. Like chapters in a novel, Dr Shukla titled every session. But, to Mugdha it seemed like that the titles were the only thing that she would get. She flipped through the pages anxiously to find something, and there it was, the first filled page in the journal.

SESSION 8.

Mugdha's eyes clenched as she devoured the contents of the session 8 and gasped,

"I know who was cremated that day!"

She quickly captured the pictures of the notes and tossed the journal opened to 'SESSION 8' to Nipun.

She dialled the number to St. Mary's asylum.

Nipun's eyes widened as he read every word from Rahul's eighth session with Dr Shukla. He pulled his hair back in disbelief as his lips silently moved with the words. He sank further into the last few pages of the session, shivering, as the phone in St. Mary's asylum rang endlessly.

Mugdha placed a call again as Nipun read the last page and collapsed on the floor next to Mugdha shaking from head to toe.

Someone answered the phone on the other end. But before Mugdha could even utter a syllable, the phone was disconnected. She looked at Nipun covered in cold sweat and grabbed his shivering hand. She gulped before she spoke.

"There was a fire at the asylum," she whispered, "Sanjana escaped and I think I know where she might have gone."

Chapter 27

Darkness had already viciously surrounded St. Mary's Asylum and the common room was beginning to look lonely. With three ward boys and a nurse, the asylum dropped its defences at night, not knowing that it would soon be under attack.

Sanjana had to create a distraction far away from where the fire would begin so that the staff did not attempt to extinguish it when it was still possible. She moved out of the common room into the toilet where she knew Dolly would have gone.

In the poorly lit bathroom, Sanjana quickly grabbed three big bottles of hand sanitizer. She poured some carefully outside Dolly's stall to make the floor slippery. She then moved towards the sink and kicked the pipe below it a few times with her bare feet. The rusty old pipe took no time to break and the water suddenly started flowing all over the common bathroom floor.

"Who is it?" asked Dolly from inside a stall.

That was Sanjana's cue to leave.

She smuggled the 3 bottles under her uniform away from the eyes of the prying staff. She carefully placed one right in front of an epileptic patient whose back would hide the bottle. She had purposefully left the bottle open anticipating him to twitch his foot in a few minutes, which would innocently knock the bottle down and would spill the flammable fluid right near the television.

She joined another patient near the window who was staring into the nothingness of the night. The window opened to the back of the asylum, into the scanty stretch of the forest. Sanjana surreptitiously removed the cap of another bottle and hid her hand behind the curtain making small conversations with the patient.

"What are you looking at?" asked Sanjana as she poured the liquid on the curtains from behind.

"The forest," said the patient, "It holds an obscure darkness within itself that even the light of a million suns cannot relinquish."

Sanjana quickly finished the bottle and threw the empty one outside the barred window.

She hid the third bottle near the couch, which she intended to use when the fire would start.

She innocently went to the staff who was chatting with each other. She started casually chatting with them, saying that she wanted to speak to someone who could actually understand and reciprocate.

She had timed everything quite perfectly. From the corner of the eye, she saw that the bottle near the TV was spilt and any moment now they would hear a loud bang from the bathroom.

And there it was, a bang followed by a painful scream. Dolly had slipped and fallen in the toilet. But, Sanjana knew that the staff would not bother to just a scream. Dolly came out, all wet, and blood dripping from her forehead.

The staff rushed to attend their favourite patient.

"The-The pipe in the bathroom is broken," she stammered, water dripping from her uniform.

Two ward boys went right away to check. The nurse took her to the emergency room to dress the open wound. The last remaining soldier went to the storeroom to get her dry clothes.

The opportunity was perfect.

Sanjana swiftly moved behind the TV and ripped the loose wires out. Sparks flew between them as she shorts them together. There was only one thing left to do, patiently wait as the heat becomes just enough to cause a fire. And voila! The corner of the carpet was consumed in flames.

She ran to the couch, grabbed the spare bottle and violently sprinkled it towards the open circuit boards on the ceiling and on the walls. She shook every last drop of the fluid out on the floor, enraging the flames.

The patients were starting to panic. Her cover was going to blow off before the fire spread more.

"Shhhh," she said loudly addressing the patients, "It's a small picnic, a bonfire to keep us warm. Let the fire grow."

She made the patients circle across the flaming carpet, sticking their hands out in flames for warmth; their backs hiding the fire.

"Bonfire...bonfire...bonfire," they chanted in a slow whisper.

Sanjana went back to where the staff had last seen her talking to them.

The ward boy from the storeroom came running in with fresh clothes and saw the patients circling something. He looked at Sanjana and she shrugged innocently like nothing had happened. The ward boy rushed to the emergency room.

Sanjana marched towards the bathroom to check on the other two ward boys. She peeped in and saw them in ankle-deep water, trying to close the main valve which was stuck because of rust.

"I came to use the bathroom," said Sanjana innocently, "But looks like I will have to wait. Can I help?"

The ward boys nodded in disagreement as one was trying to stop the water leak from the broken pipe with his hands and another was trying to shut the main valve.

Sanjana went back into the common room.

"Let the fire grow... let the fire grow," whispered another schizophrenic patient, looking into the now burning curtain as he threw heaps of old newspapers into the fire.

The flames had become violent now, almost brushing the ceiling. The place felt hot like a furnace. The entire room was caught in the inferno.

The staff attending Dolly came inside after sedating her in the emergency room.

The fire on the ceiling crept through the wires and exploded as it hit the circuit box, consuming more of the room in flames.

The fire was spreading and now the patients started to panic again.

The ward boy loudly called for the other 2 staff members and shouted to take everyone out to safety, which meant, the doors to the criminal wards were going to be opened.

That was a golden opportunity for Sanjana. As planned, she offered to help by taking a few patients outside in the compound. The understaffed asylum had no other choice. The exit doors were open, and the docile patients did not require assistance or monitoring.

Sanjana escorted 2 patients out first, coughing terribly after having inhaled a lot of smoke.

The security guards stood in attention.

"Please...Please help," coughed Sanjana collapsing on the floor, forcing the other two patients with her on the floor as well, "There is a big fire inside...please."

The gates were securely locked, and the compound was too tall for anyone to jump over it. There was nothing to worry about, thought the guards as they went inside.

Sanjana stopped coughing and made a run for her life. She sprinted with Manu's mental image in her head, his bruised face and how he needed her help. She could tell that the fire inside had grown. Perhaps the fools tried to extinguish an electric fire with water. Her feet came to a halt in front for the hole in the compound wall that Manu had talked about. The orange lit asylum cast a big shadow into the dark. Sanjana took a final look at the raging hellfire, into the heart of the burning devil and smiled.

She squeezed herself through the hole, venturing from the blazing heat to the cold darkness of the forest. All she had to do was keep running straight and then she would meet the main road.

As her feet felt the mush of the black earth, the soft soil acted like it wanted her to escape. The trees had cleared her path and the moon was shining brighter than the sun. She knew where she was heading. It seemed like the whole universe was cheering for her and wanted her to reunite with her one true love- her son, to satisfy the one true purpose of her life, to be able to be the best mother she could be.

As nature silently screamed, 'Run Sanjana Run' at the brim of the forest, where the road met, a silhouette silently stood there for Sanjana.

Sanjana came to a stop, out in the open with tears in her eyes.

The silhouette turned around with new clothes in her hand. As the moon shone his luminescence on her face, there she stood, facing Sanjana with the kindest eyes; the same disfigured woman from the temple- bent spine, covered in a rug, poverty-stricken, but immense kindness in her eyes.

"Take these," she said softly as she offered her fresh set of clothes, "Take this, beta. Change from your patient uniform; otherwise, no one will give you a ride back home."

Sanjana silently obliged.

The old lady reached for her pouch and grabbed some money from it.

"Here, take it for the taxi," she said.

She locked Sanjana in a warm embrace like she was exuding motherly feelings to her. As she broke the embrace, Sanjana saw that the woman's eyes were wet.

"Why are you crying?" asked Sanjana feeling emotional.

"You go now," said the woman in a broken whisper, tucking Sanjana's hair behind her ear, "Go, darling, it's the night of the moon. Everything will be fine. Go and reunite with your family."

She kissed Sanjana on her forehead as Sanjana waved at a passing taxi. Sanjana could not believe how everything was just falling in place that night. She sat in the taxi, thinking of how unlikely it was to find one there at that hour.

She looked out to wave goodbye, but the woman was nowhere to be seen.

After many doorbells, Ratna opened the door to find Sanjana standing in the doorframe with ash all over her face, muddy feet, red eyes, and shivering from head to toe. She collapsed right there and began to cry loudly.

Ratna picked her up and hugged her daughter, escorting her in the living room. She tried to rub her arms, but Sanjana was dangerously cold. Ratna made her sit on the couch and ran inside her bedroom to return with blankets. She tucked her daughter inside.

"Honey, I am going to make you hot tea," said Ratna with concern moving quickly into the kitchen, "I will be back in a minute, darling."

Sanjana shivered inside the blanket as she spoke, "Where is dad? And where is Manu?"

Her mother called for her father from the kitchen and said, "He is taking a shower."

Before Ratna could speak more, an unattended phone rang on the table in front of the couch.

Ratna shouted again for her husband, telling him that his phone was ringing.

A peculiar name flashed on the screen next to Sanjana.

Punit Calling...

As the phone stopped ringing, Sanjana grabbed the phone in her hands to check for what she dreaded she would see. She scrolled through the call logs to find 15 missed calls of Punit, and there popped a chat notification.

3 unread messages from Punit.

She opened the messages as tears rolled down her eyes.

'Answer your phone.'

'I don't think I can pretend anymore.'

'We have just reached stage 3, prepare for stage 4.'

Chapter 28

As Sanjana's father stood behind her watching her drown in her tears, she tried to speak between her sobs.

"Why- the-hell-is-Punit-calling-you?"

Her mother placed a hand on her shoulder and offered her warm tea, but she refused to take it. Instead, she embraced her mother as tightly as she could and cried loudly at the betrayal. Her mother gently caressed her back, tearing up herself.

"It's okay, beta," said Ratna, "Let it out... Cry loudly if you want. I am right here."

She stroked her hair as Sanjana wailed at the misery her life seemed to be. The universe that seemed to be in tandem with her suddenly seemed against her.

"Why?" her voice cracked as she asked, "Why dad? Why?"

Her father couldn't speak. He just watched Sanjana cry as his heart pounded outside his chest. He did not know what to tell her that would even begin to make her feel good. He finally mustered some courage and uttered his first words to her.

"Sanju, Punit is just trying to help you," he completed covered with sweat.

Sanjana picked her head up from her mother's shoulder, looked her dad in the eye and chewed every word she chose to say,

"Help me? Help me with what? That bastard is replacing everyone around me."

Her father did not answer. His hand started shivering as he looked to the floor.

Her mother grabbed his hand and looked into Sanjana's eyes with compassion.

"Sanju," she said lovingly.

Her father signalled her to stop, but Ratna continued.

"Sanju... beta, you are very very sick... you need help. We are all just trying to help you."

"Bullshit, mom," snapped Sanju, "You would rather believe what that imposter has to say about me than your own daughter. Shame on you."

"He-He is not an imposter," said her father, "He is the real Punit."

"Oh yes?" said Sanjana rhetorically, "You were there when he died all those years ago. You were there when he was cremated. You carried him on your shoulders. And now, for some reason, you are suddenly blind to all this."

She saw both her parents had teared up.

"And you, mom? You were in this whole plan too? Proving your own daughter insane. Making me believe that I am some kind of a nutcase who belongs in that hell hole, where, by the way, I got assaulted."

Her mother's eyes widened at the bruises on her neck.

"Oh my God!" she gasped," Who did this to you, Sanju?"

"Does that even matter?" Sanjana replied back scornfully, "It all happened when my incompetent father was taking an imposter home, who by the way, abused your grandchild."

"She did what?" exclaimed her father.

"Manu... he came with bruises all over his face and a cut lip."

"We- We did not visit the asylum, honey," said Ratna, "There is no other woman. Like there is no other Punit. Just you, just Punit."

Sanjana's head went for a toss. She closed her eyes tightly, trying to squeeze every tear out of them. Then she opened them to face her mother and spoke confidently,

"You are trying to prove it to me that I am mad," her eyes bulged out as she spoke marching towards her father with his phone, "Everyone is fucking involved. Manu warned me, and he was right. Everyone is fucking involved."

"Manu..." she yelled loudly, "Manu... come downstairs right now. We are leaving. Manu..."

She brought the phone to her father's nose, shoving it in.

"And what...what- is... is.... what... what the fuck is this Stage 2 and Stage 4," she stammered uncannily.

Her father stood there avoiding eye contact at all costs as he whispered in his broken voice,

"They are the five stages of grief. It was to help you process the loss."

"Aha..." jumped Sanjana as her eyes shrunk and her pupils dilated, "What loss? You just said that this Punit is the real Punit. If you said the truth before, there is no loss to process, is there? Caught you."

Sanjana laughed hysterically as her parents were silenced by her argument.

"Let me tell you why this can't be the real Punit," said Sanjana slowly marching towards her mother. She leaned into her, tucked her hair behind her ear, and slowly, but loudly, whispered into it, "You know why? It is because I killed him."

She retracted, piercing Ratna's gaze.

Ratna's chin wobbled before she spoke.

"But darling, you didn't," said her mother trying to hold her face in her hands, "You didn't kill Punit. Stop living in that guilt. He is not dead. He is alive and loves you very much. He has spent hours of sleepless nights to even get you better. He has studied all books on psychology there are to bring you back. He loves you, darling, much more than we all do. Please come out of this, Sanju."

There was a strange genuineness in her mother's voice. What if she really needed help? What if she really had Capgras Delusion? But what if the parents in front of here were imposters too?

Reality seemed like a big blur to her, the mist around which refused to clear no matter how hard she tried. There were still so many things that did not make sense about all of this.

"Why the hell would my Punit then try to hurt Manu? Why the hell would he do that to his own son? Why the hell would he wait for ten years to show himself and let me raise Manu all on my own?"

Her parents went silent again.

"You all were there. I remember. I couldn't have made up an entire funeral in my head." she cried, but there was also so much anger in her sadness, "If these really are stages of grief, what loss am I going through?"

She sat down on the couch, pulling her hair back, trying not to cry at all.

"Manu..." she screamed louder that time, "Where is he?"

"He is not here," said her mother.

Flashes of Manu's bruised face came before Sanjana as she stared on the floor.

"Why wait for ten years?" Sanjana's voice squeaked as if her vocal cords had begun to bleed.

Her mother grabbed her by the wrist and dragged her near a mirror.

"Look at yourself, Sanju," said her mother with concern, "You have barely even aged..."

"Ratna..." warned her father, but she ignored.

"I can't see her like this," cried her mother wiping Sanjana's face with her saree, "Beta, there was a funeral, and it is barely even a year after that... look at you...look at us... we have barely aged..."

"Ratna, that's enough," scolded her father.

Sanjana frantically touched her face and realised the truth in her mother's voice. How could it be? Flashes of Manu's bruised face appeared before her eyes. She was physically present there, but her thoughts kept roaming around, raising Manu all alone all those years.

Her fond memories of little Manu and her, laughing and arguing filled her eyes. She pursued her lips to exhale cold air as she forced a big smile into the mirror, wiping her tears constantly. Her mind suddenly flashed the memory of a fifteen-year-old Manu, with a bruised face, outside her asylum saying,

"Mom, no power in this universe can fool me from recognising my mother. It is only you whom I trust, and nothing ever will part us."

Sanjana's smile turned into a crestfallen frown as she exhaled loudly through her mouth and grief channelled its way out through a stream of uncontrollable tears.

She walked around with the stooped spine whispering to herself. She quickly grabbed the keys to her father's car, knocked the sofa on her way and ran directly to the car.

Her parents took some time to move through the obstacles she had created, but as they got out, Sanjana sped the accelerator and knocked their front gate down in full speed.

"Thanks, mom, dad," she waved at them momentarily with a sadness they had never seen before, "But I need to save my son."

And she zoomed into the dark.

Ratna tried to run after her, but her husband stopped her.

"It's too late, Ratna," he said, wiping his tears with his sleeves, "She has already crossed stage 4. She should not be forced to remember that Manu died that night before she is in Stage 5."

"We need to call Punit immediately," said Ratna.

Sanjana parked her father's car in front of her house. She hurried towards the gate where Mugdha was already waiting for her with an envelope.

"Ma'am," inhaled Mugdha touching her arm gently.

She gave her the envelope, gulped, and spoke.

"This envelope has the entire truth. It also has a cheque with the entire amount you gave me. I can't take it..."

Mugdha pressed her shoulder and walked away. She gave a last look to Sanjana with clenched eyebrows and said,

"I am so sorry, ma'am. Goodbye."

Chapter 29

"Welcome to your eighth session, Rahul," said Dr Shukla as he opened the door for his patient to come in.

The previous seven sessions had not thrown any light on Rahul. He always came for the sessions on time, didn't speak anything, sat on the couch for his 45 minutes staring at random things in the room and left with a smile. Dr Shukla always thought that the next session would be different from the previous. He tried using several methods to instigate a reaction in his 'mute' patient, but nothing had worked. The room was always filled with depressing silence or with Dr Shukla's unanswered questions.

Despite all that, Rahul showed up regularly. He booked weekly appointments with such discipline as if something about Dr Shukla was really helping him. But that was not enough for the psychiatrist. Rahul showed visible signs of depression at times, but he never said anything explicitly. This was the last attempt Dr Shukla had planned to get Rahul speaking.

Like every other session, Rahul sat on the couch directly. However, Dr Shukla, instead of making conversation with Rahul, or even acknowledging his presence, sat across his desk with '*Pride and Prejudice*' opened in front of him.

"Are we sitting here today?" asked Rahul.

Dr Shukla raised his finger to silence Rahul, with his head still buried in his book.

Rahul gulped and sat still on the sofa, looking at the ceiling. There was absolute silence in the room, when suddenly Dr Shukla broke it, reading aloud,

"She began now to comprehend that he was exactly the man who, in disposition and talents, would most suit her. His understanding and temper, though unlike her own..."

"What is this?" said Rahul meekly.

Dr Shukla noticed the first sign of reaction. He again raised his finger and continued reading, burying his head further into the pages of the timeless tale.

"It was a union that must have been to the advantage of both; by her ease and liveliness, his mind might have been softened..."

"What is going on?" Rahul enquired loudly that time, clearing his throat.

A second sign of reaction.

Dr Shukla continued.

"A union of a different tendency, and precluding the possibility of the other, was soon to be formed in their family..."

Rahul was visibly enraged now. He balled his fist, smacked it on the couch and stood up. His face had become completely red, eyes tearing up as he yelled,

"You won't give a damn about your patient, and you'd rather read your novel. Look at me!"

There was a third sign. But the psychiatrist knew that stopping now would mean that Rahul would just go back into his shell. He was on the fence. He just needed to be tipped a little more.

Dr Shukla continued, ignoring all signs of rage.

"But how little of permanent happiness could belong to a couple who were only brought together because..."

"Look at me," cried Rahul, "Help me... please."

"...their passions were stronger than their virtue, she could easily conjecture..."

"Please," begged Rahul, "I don't know what to do…or where to go."

He crouched on the floor near the lamp and buried his head in his knees, crying.

"Everything is wrong…everything. And I… I have nothing left… It was my mistake."

Dr Shukla silently opened Rahul's journal and wrote on a fresh page in all capitals- SESSION 8.

"Please," Rahul's voice broke as he looked at the doctor and fell to the floor burying his face in his trembling hands, screaming, "No…no…no…"

Dr Shukla picked him and escorted him to the couch.

"I've lost everything," whispered Rahul in sobs, lightly punching his eyes.

Dr Shukla knew not to interrupt him and let him bleed his heart out.

"I lied… My real name is Punit," drops of tears fell from his eyes to the floor for the first time. He always let them well up, but never let them fall. He wiped them every second as his lips tremored with every word he spoke.

"Eight months ago, my wife and I lost our five-year-old son, Abhimanyu. He was this sweet little happy kid…ver-very intelligent, but a little fragile. I…I always," he looked up, clenched his eyebrows, wiped his nose with his palms and exhaled through his mouth.

"It's so hard…." he cried, trying to contain himself, continuously exhaling through his pursed lips, "I always wanted to toughen him up. I wanted to prepare him for the brutal real world, which is unkind and hurtful. Manu had some food allergies, especially fish. That night, I purposefully got fried fish for us. I was forcing Manu to at least try one morsel, but Sanju warned me not to give it to him. You see, Manu and I never had the relationship I imagined we would have. I was emotionally unavailable as a father. All my efforts into toughening up distanced me from my own son. My sweet boy tried his best to impress me always, but I was too strict. That-that night, after Sanju stopped me from feeding him fish, I did not insist. Manu may have seen the look of disappointment on my face, I think. So, when Sanju and I were picking the dishes after dinner, he secretly had one morsel of fish.

Later that night, Sanju put Manu to sleep and went to have a bath. I was watching TV. I heard sounds of furniture shifting from Manu's bedroom. He had always complained about the wobbly bed, but I never cared to fix it. Sanju came out of the bathroom, all alarmed and wet. She was going upstairs to check on Manu, but I told her that her overprotectiveness is just going to make him weaker. She was reluctant to listen to me, but then she stood there at the end of our stairs, contemplating. And then we heard a lamp breaking in his room. That was enough. Sanju sprinted to his bedroom leaving behind a trail of water. I rushed behind her, but I slipped and fell at the top of the stairs. When I reached his room, Manu's half body was hanging upside down from the bed. And Sanju couldn't think of what to do. His head was close to the floor and he was not breathing. Her world had turned upside down. My son had an anaphylactic shock. The poor boy was struggling for air and I chose to ignore him..." his constant sniffing stopped as he let the tears storm out in heartbreaking sobs.

"We picked Manu up. Sanju cried and cried and cried for help. I immediately called a family doctor home. Sanju vigorously shook him to wake him up. We started giving him chest compressions. His little t-shirt sleeve got caught in my watch and a piece of fabric ripped off, but my cub didn't move. I knew he had passed already, but there was that tiny hope that he will suddenly jump back to life and grab a book and ask us to read it to him. He was just five and a half and had to go through so much. Just because of that one stupid idea that I had. The doctor arrived and declared him dead. If that wasn't painful enough, Sanju's loud wail was something I have still been unable to forget. I sat shivering on a chair in the corner, in that dark room lit by the passage light. Sanju still wouldn't give up and kept shaking Manu for two whole hours. She called her mother in sobs, lay next to Manu and kept stroking his hair.

"Sanju, I will call the rest of the family," I said to her.

"You are dead to me. You did this," she said back to me.

I did not have the courage to face her. She wasn't wrong. I did do this. I am responsible for the death of my own child. Sanju lay there next to him the whole night as I called our family members. I returned to see Sanju singing our dead child a lullaby. I tried stopping her, but she angrily snapped at me every time, breaking into sobs. Next morning, when my parents arrived, we picked Manu up and got him downstairs.

Sanju had spent the whole night in her wet clothes, shivering with cold, refusing to move or to let Manu out of sight. Her tear ducts had dried up and she couldn't cry anymore. She barely even moved. When my mother arrived, Sanjana wailed in her embrace dropping words from sentences, not making sense at all. My mother was very close to Manu but watching Sanju like that broke her completely. We waited for Sanju's parents to arrive who were not in town at that time. When they did, we all sat for *puja* and began the rituals. Sanju just sat near the corpse the whole time holding her mother's hand. She had not spoken anything in hours but when her dad told her that we were going to take the body away, she finally spoke.

She followed our van to the crematorium on foot. When she was there, she saw the entire thing from a distance and then when everyone left, she sat there near the burning pyre the whole night. I sat there too, right next to her, but didn't say a word. In the morning, she got up and threw her *mangalsutra* into the fire, I reached into the hot logs of wood to retrieve it, burning my hand in the process. She began walking away. I asked her if she didn't want to wait for me, but she ran away.

Do you know doc, how it is to collect the ashes of your five-year-old? There isn't anything left that you can identify him with. Dispersing his ashes was the toughest thing I have done in life. And until today, I refused to revisit that day.

When I came back home, after dispersing the ashes and dropping our parents, everything in the house screamed of Manu. The things, the smell, everything reminded me of him. I finally decided to fix his bed that he had always complained about. I grabbed a hammer, went up to his room to fix everything, and I realised I had not cried at all. I buried my head in his pillow and cried as loudly as I could yelling out his name. When I came down, I saw Sanju's phone on the cabinet with Manu's favourite game on it, that he would always play. I lost it. I smashed her phone with the hammer and threw the *mangalsutra* in my hand away.

Sanju had stopped acknowledging me completely. I did not realise that she had begun to take 'you're dead to me' so seriously. Whenever I slept in the same bed, she would get up randomly at night and go to Manu's bedroom to sleep. She was not ready to get over Manu. She had started talking to walls and empty spaces.

Once, she was in our room with Manu's favourite teddy bear in her lap. She was singing it the same lullaby. She had not slept for days, she looked dreadful. I told her to snap out of it, but she became violent and ripped the bear apart with her bare hands. In that chaos, our cat, Poe, got scared and clawed Sanju near the neck. She was bleeding and still, she asked me to stay away. I tried to hold her, but she cried and refused and ran to Manu's room.

My mother is a clinical psychologist. She realised that Sanju was hallucinating since the morning of the funeral itself. We decided to let her take time to process the loss through five stages of grief. In that process, forcing the information of

Manu's death could be dangerous for her and could possibly tip her over the brink of sanity.

So, I moved out of her way. Did not speak, did not show my existence. Every day, I saw my wife getting more and more involved in her hallucinations. She even celebrated Manu's birthdays with my parents and her parents, but we had to play along for her to process the loss. We had to; otherwise, wrong timing could make things worse.

She had lost all sense of time and space. I got my head buried in books on psychology trying to help my one source of light left in the house. It affected my work, I started randomly skipping work, spoke things like 'I am planning my funeral' with some colleagues. They even termed me absconded, but I didn't care. Sanju was more important to me. She was so deep in the denial stage that she even burned Manu's death certificate and kept the ashes in the safe.

But I was terrified when her hallucinations started to grow. She made up a character of Manu's teacher. She picked some dead university professor from the obituary in the newspapers. And I knew that I couldn't watch her do that to herself. So, from the months of observation of her patterns of when she would not be hallucinating, I decided to show myself. When she saw me, she froze in her place for 20 minutes before she could even speak. When she did speak, she spoke gibberish. Dropped a lot of words from her sentences and we realised that her schizophrenia had turned catatonic.

My mom had suggested her to see you, for her nightmares and my voices that she ignored to hear and thought that I was a ghost. I came to you because I wanted to know how Sanju was doing, clicking pictures of your patient notes of Sanjana."

Dr Shukla silently wrote everything as his heart sank for both his patients.

"Things became even more complicated when it all developed into Capgras Delusion. She refused to recognise me. I tried, I tried to make her believe that I was really her husband, her Punit, with whom she fell in love with. But everything was futile," Punit sobbed, "But if it means that she will get better, she will get to stage 5, I am willing to dissolve from her life. Every breath I take feels poisonous. Everything I touch rots. Tell me, sir, what should I do? Please... I can't…I tried to be so strong, tried to be the pillar of my family, or whatever is left of it. But I just can't anymore. I am losing all my strength every day, like I am hitting a dead-end and still I keep smacking my head against it hoping that the end in front of me is just a paper wall that will one day tear, and from the other end I will be able to get my wife back from the traps of her hallucinations. That day, I will sleep, that day I will know that there is a God, and that day I will be able to forgive myself."

Dr Shukla sighed. He had two children and he could feel Punit's pain.

"Punit," said the psychiatrist comforting him, "I agree with my colleague. We will let Sanjana get to stage 5 on her own. We will have to be patient. It must be natural in all aspects. Anything forced will have dire consequences."

Punit looked at Dr Shukla with his slaughtered soul. A painstaking desperateness reflected in his tired eyes.

"I just want my family back."

Chapter 30

Sanjana leafed through the printouts of Dr Shukla's notes that Mugdha had presented her. She sat on the front porch, with her head buried in the papers, every syllable stabbing her heart. As she flipped through the last page, afraid to blink with lashes that bore the weight of her tears, a wall that she had erected had fallen. There was one last thing in that envelope- a familiar receipt from the crematorium. The only difference that time was that now the receipt had the missing gaps filled in.

Name of the deceased- Abhimanyu Poddar

Gender- Male

Age- 5.5 years

A cold breeze brushed the back of her neck, eerily comforting her trembling body. She dropped the envelope outside and rushed into the house. She closed the door behind her, entering the carcass of the abode.

She closed her eyes, and flashes of the night she killed Poe came haunting back to her. In that moment of terror, she fearfully opened her eyes with nothing but white noise in her head. She looked around and physically felt the petrifying sound of loneliness, that beckoned as if nothing existed in the universe anymore. As her eyes closed, flashes of her son appeared before her, running bare feet behind her on the road to the crematorium.

She quickly climbed the flight of stairs to enter her bedroom. As the closet door opened, a white saree lay at the bottommost compartment, neatly tucked in.

Sanjana unfolded the entire saree that she had refused to wash for what she felt was 10 years. It was the same saree she had worn to the crematorium. She frantically searched the dusty white fabric of her saree, hoping to find tiny mud marks from when she had wiped off Manu's feet. But there was nothing.

"I...I remember... I remember I did," she whispered loudly as a dam holding her tears suddenly collapsed.

She brought the saree to her nose and inhaled the fragrance of the love she had lost that day. It smelled like smoke, it smelled like death, but there was one smell that overpowered any other scent, it smelled like the five-year-old Manu.

She picked herself up, clutched the saree close to her chest, wetting it with the rain of loss pouring from her eyes and came out in the passage.

As she scanned the hollow mansion with quivering lips and eyes that refused to let any more tears roll down, at the bottom of the staircase stood a fifteen-year-old boy, dressed in angelic white, silently looking at her.

Sanjana's lips involuntarily lifted themselves up into a gentle smile. She kept her eyes wide open, absorbing her son's light, afraid to blink. What if he went away?

Manu walked towards the table and sat down with his books in front of him. He quietly made long strokes with his pen on an open notebook.

Sanjana tilted her head to look at Manu with pride.

"Shall I get you some juice?" she asked.

But he didn't respond. He just quietly sat there, as if frozen in time, repeating his actions over and again.

As she descended the stairs looking at Manu, her feet wobbled. The end of the stairs was getting brighter with every step she took. As she stepped into that blinding brightness, her eyes burned no more from the tears.

Everything in the house was clean, untouched with a golden glow like nothing had ever happened there. Poe jumped from behind the couch, gently purring as she approached Sanjana. She rubbed herself between Sanjana's feet, lovingly and then jumped onto a chair beside Manu.

Sanjana sat in the chair in front of Manu.

"You look so handsome," said Sanjana with moist eyes, "Or at least you would have looked this handsome."

Manu was still making long strokes on his notebook when he suddenly stopped.

"Oh no…no….no, baby. I didn't mean to interrupt," said Sanjana, "Continue to study…"

Manu looked up at his mother with tearful eyes and he smiled at her. He took Sanjana's hands in his icy cold hands and said,

"You can never interrupt me, mom. And I am so proud of you…" he broke into tears, but his smile was constant, "You made it out of that asylum, mom. I am so proud."

Sanjana's hands shivered in his.

"You were always cold…" she said, "All these years. Your body was always so cold… like…"

"Like there was no life left in me," laughed Manu.

Sanjana bit her lower lip looking at her handsome prince feeling the warmth of his icy touch.

"I…I have so many questions," she said innocently.

"I will help you answer them, mom," said a voice from behind her.

As she looked behind, a thirteen-year-old stood in front of her with his arms stretched out for a hug. Sanjana looked back at the desk and her son at the table had disappeared.

She slowly stood up and hugged Manu's cold body.

"What is it, mom?" said the thirteen-year-old holding his mother's hand and looking up at her with moist eyes and a smile.

"We-We celebrated your birthday," said Sanjana looking at Manu.

"And yet no one else ever fed me the cake," said Manu.

"But all those years of study and notes?"

"Mom, don't you find that my handwriting is exactly the same as yours?"

Manu moved away from her and picked up Poe in his hand, gently stroking her below the chin.

"Why do I have to wear dad's clothes always?" heard Sanjana from the bathroom.

As her neck turned momentarily towards the voice, Manu had disappeared.

Poe slowly walked towards the bathroom, guiding Sanjana. As Sanjana opened the bathroom door, she saw a ten-year-old Manu sitting on the floor, looking down sadly.

"What is the matter, beta?" asked Sanjana, passing her fingers through his hair in concern. Her heart bleeding from the stabs of reality.

"I always have to wear dad's clothes, never new ones," scoffed the ten-year-old Manu.

Sanjana realised that she had always imagined Manu in Punit's clothes.

Manu quickly got up, took Sanjana's hands and pulled her into the living room happily. He gave her his notebook.

Sanjana opened the notebook and gasped.

It was filled with unintelligible strokes. Every page had just scribbles on it. As she closed her eyes momentarily, flashes of her sitting alone at the desk, scribbling on the book appeared before her. It felt like something had crawled under her skin and squeezed her very heart. She dropped the book to look at Manu, but he was gone.

Her hands hung from her shoulders to the side, eyes desperate for the sight of her son, when a cold little hand held her finger from behind. She looked down, and there he was, her six-year-old, innocently smiling looking into her eyes. Like he had never seen anyone braver, smarter or more beautiful than her. His eyes screamed of unconditional love for his mother. He looked at her with such safety, like nothing in the world would ever be able to harm him if he kept looking at her.

He hugged her with his tiny body, reaching only her legs. He swayed with her side to side, as if dancing. His small feet were resting on his mother's feet. Sanjana could see his happy face looking at her, his innocent eyes gleaming with a sense of security and shelter in his mother's warmth. She bent down to kiss him, but he was gone.

The main door creaked open. Sanjana looked around to notice a young man sitting on the front porch, holding the yellow envelope, with his back towards the house. Sanjana sat next to him.

He looked a lot like Punit, just younger, like in his early twenties. He was crying looking at the abundantly starlit sky holding the crematorium receipt in his hand. He rested his head on Sanjana's shoulder, still looking up. His eyes were swept with tears.

"Mom," he said in almost a whisper, "When I was little, you told me that every tear I shed becomes a star. Look, mom, there is no more space left in the sky today."

Every time she cried, she gave away a piece of her to the universe, and she had nothing more left to give as she looked at the sky holding Manu's cold hand.

"Now you know everything, mom."

"But-but, you helped me escape," stammered Sanjana slightly confused, pressing Manu's hand gently.

"Mom, you are the most intelligent person I have known. You were observant when the van got you to the asylum. You noticed every single thing by yourself. I was just a mere figment of your imagination, a driving force to keep you going."

"H-how?" sobbed Sanjana, "How? I don't understand. You were with me all the time whenever I spoke to people too."

"Think again, mom. No one ever interacted directly with me. The policeman never saw me, dad kept asking you where I was, in the asylum, you saw me just standing separately beside everyone else, and you already know about Dr Kartik through your doctor's notes."

Sanjana squeezed Manu's hand tightly.

"I-I am so sorry. I failed you," said Sanjana, as her tears fell on the already damp saree she was clutching.

"No-no-no mom," consoled Manu looking at Sanjana, "You never once failed me. Look at me, mom."

He cupped her face in his hands, kissed her on her forehead and said,

"I have been nothing but proud of you, mom. So proud that no book on psychology would be able to express this feeling with any science. You always wanted to see me grow up, and you did. It was irrelevant if I was real to others or not. I was real for you; the experience was real for you, and the rest is just empty spaces between words."

Sanjana looked at him, finding it difficult to breathe between her sobs and the heartache. She looked into his eyes, still innocent, still the same that her five-year-old had. Her pupils moved around to absorb every inch of his face before he faded away, to etch him forever in her memory.

"Is-is there heaven?" asked Sanjana looking at the stars that paraded the night.

Manu looked at his mother and smiled.

"Yes, mom, there is," he said, placing his head on her lap, "It is right here, with you."

As Manu stared into the dark of the garden in his mother's lap, he knew there was nowhere else in the world he wanted to be.

"Did the cremation hurt?" asked Sanjana gently rocking Manu in her lap as the sky got brighter.

"Not even a little," replied Manu getting up, "Remember how in the nightmares we shared, the fire could never hurt me. In fact, nothing hurts anymore."

He picked up Sanjana in his arms like a child, carrying her inside. The glow in the room wiped off as he walked across the house with his mother in his arms, unveiling the brutal reality every step.

"Remember how you used to carry me upstairs to my room when I got tired and slept anywhere," said Manu looking at his mother in his arms, climbing the stairs, "I always wanted to do that for you when you got old."

They entered Manu's bedroom where a five-year-old Manu was sitting upright on his bed. Sanjana found herself standing in the doorframe, looking at her baby boy presenting her with his ripped off teddy bear. The older Manu was gone. She looked down at her hands; they were holding a needle and thread.

She sat beside Manu, sewing the ripped off bear as Manu watched her with the purest smile. The tenderness of her tears washing the horrors attached to the toy away. He took the perfectly sewn bear from her and lay on his bed hugging it, trying to fall asleep.

"Sing me a lullaby, mom," said a voice from behind her.

All her the phases of her son who had progressed over the years were leaning on her with their eyes closed, her five-year-old was next to her in the same place where he had passed, and her fifteen-year-old was with his head in her lap.

"Mom," said her twenty-something old Manu standing in the doorframe as he looked at all his phases of life sleeping near Sanjana, "It's time for me to go. You know everything now. Let me sleep."

"I can't say goodbye," said Sanjana looking at everyone. "What if I want to be in this hallucination? What if I want this to be my reality? I can't lose you. Not again."

"You won't lose me, mom," said the oldest Manu, standing beside his bed, eyes filled with sorrow, but a smile radiating on his face, "I am in here," he pointed at her heart, "And I must sleep now...I am so tired."

Sanjana knew that it was goodbye, but if it meant for her to suffer for the happiness and comfort of her child, she was willing to go through it.

She walked into the mess of Manu's books, picked up a notebook and a pen and sat on the bed again.

"I don't want to forget this at all," said Sanjana, looking at all of them with a smile, "Don't worry, it will be over soon."

"Thanks mom," said the five-year-old Manu.

She kissed his cold forehead, closed her eyes and began humming Manu's favourite lullaby. She kept rocking her lap and swaying her head side to side. There was an unusual warmth that surrounded her, like her son's cold body, was finally warming with her love.

As she opened her eyes, everyone else was gone except the sewn-up teddy bear, sleeping next to her in place of her son. She stroked the bear and said,

"I can't let you be alone," and began writing something.

As she kept writing in the almost darkness of the yellow night lamp in Manu's room, on his bed, the parade of the lights in the sky began to disappear, perhaps for eternity.

Chapter 31

Punit's car came to a screeching stop in front of the Poddar mansion after receiving a call from Sanjana's father and the mental asylum.

He ran out of his car straight to the gate, his heart beating outside his chest anticipating the worst. In his sprint he ignored a disfigured old lady sitting on the footpath right opposite to their lavish abode, crying in silence.

On the porch, he bent down to examine loose pieces of paper and a receipt from the crematorium.

"No-no-no-no," cried Punit, pulling his hair back.

He immediately broke the door open and scanned the monstrous house. The silence in the dark shrieked of cold emptiness, like the very heart of the house had flatlined, like it had sacrificed itself in the embrace of grief.

"Sanju…" yelled Punit, shivering from head to toe in fear, like every muscle of his body had been massacred, "Sanju… Sanjana."

He rushed upstairs breathing heavily through his mouth, his throat narrowing every step on the way. He stood in front of Manu's bedroom, switched on the lights, and fell to his knees right at the doorframe.

Sanjana lay on the bed in a white saree, hugging Manu's sewn-up teddy bear, with an empty packet of Punit's blood pressure pills. She looked like she was sleeping peacefully, with a gentle smile of satisfaction on her face.

No more nightmares, no more hallucinations, just peace.

Punit's mouth opened involuntarily as he howled in pain. He crawled to her, shook her vigorously.

"Sanju...please wake up. Sanju... please don't leave me. Please wake up. I will not trouble you any more, I promise."

He quickly called an ambulance in sobs still violently shaking her stiff body. Her temples had gone cold, and her heart had gone mute.

"I promise I will go away, Sanju. You were right, I am an imposter...but please come back."

He picked her head and brought her close to his chest screaming in that empty house,

"Help me... someone help me...anyone...Help..."

His blurry eyes looked at her happy face, his fingers entangled in her hair when he noticed an open notebook lying lifeless beside her. He grabbed the book, flipped through its pages and began reading-

'I thought I knew what love and care meant. I thought I knew what I was doing. I thought I was brave and strong, but I have never been more wrong in my life.

Punit, you taught me what it feels like to be loved. You taught me how to love. You gave me Manu, which was the greatest gift I could ever get; so great that the absence of that gift created an endless void in me. When reality hit me, it felt like someone slit my throat and left me open to bleed.

I don't know what is going to happen. Is there a light or just endless cold darkness? Do I become a star in the sky or just ashes in the river? Is there a new beginning or this is the end? But I know one thing for sure, that I'll never have to say goodbye to my boy again.

But please read this not as a note of an ending, but like an apology that you deserve from me.

Stage 1- Denial

I don't know where to begin. Let me start by telling you how sorry I am. I constantly felt like I was being choked to death with flashes of in and out of my reality. I am sorry that I denied your existence.

I am sorry that I put the blame of Manu's death on you. I don't feel the same any more. If it makes any difference, or if I am worth saying this, I forgive you. And don't hold yourself responsible even for a jiffy about anything.

You are the definition of the perfect husband. I just wasn't a good enough wife.

Stage 2- Anger

I can't help blaming myself for everything. As I close my eyes, flashes of Poe haunt me. The very cat that comforted me, I did not even hesitate to kill. If possible, please forgive me.

Every time I think about it, a black hole opens sucking me deep inside my darkness, like my conscience has died silently under my skin, and raging anger takes over me; anger not at anyone but myself. This never-ending feeling of self-hate that brings me to the cusp of tears, like nothing good will ever exist in me anymore, like one day, I will suddenly wake up and find myself surrounded by hellfire.

But with me, shall fade my anger. I promise of taking away this demon forever from your life.

Stage 3- Bargaining

Isn't it ironic how I did all this to protect my family when this itself became the reason why we stand as three isolated pillars today than as a triangle? Huh. Like shards of glass, my memories are scattered all over this house. They are in so many tiny pieces, that it became impossible for me to find them all. I tried piecing them all together, but it is just too difficult.

It's so hard!

I could have given anything to get us all back together, but it seems like this is the price I must pay, but at least now I will be with him.

Stage 4- Depression

When I started believing that you were gone, and I began manufacturing my nightmares through our reality, some part of me still knew that wasn't real. I built such a thick wall around the reality that I no longer knew what was happening.

I know this made you very sad but let me wash my sins in your tears today. All the things that you tried to do to make me better, paid off. Please don't try to understand my sadness, because sometimes it takes birth in such a deep place that by the time it surfaces, you only see mere drops in the eyes, but the sea inside remains hidden.

In your eyes, Punit, I saw a light. A light that I wish I knew was there to help me, a light I wish I knew was divine and not infernal. I wish...I wish so many things, but most importantly, I wish that you live a happy life.

Stage 5- Acceptance

I never stopped loving you, even when I was angry at you, and not even now. When I thought you were an imposter, I started to fall in love with you all over again. I felt so guilty like I was cheating on my dead husband. The feelings were so complicated to understand that my reality became even more difficult to grasp and it was even easier to live inside my imaginations.

I accept that I wronged you... all of you. You, your parents, my parents... everyone. But I know for sure, that there wasn't even a single instance, where I stopped loving any of you. Accept my apology as the only form of love I am capable of giving to you right now.

I know you know that I don't believe in God, but as I prayed and prayed for us, for Manu, I think I met God or maybe she, too, was my hallucination. There was this old disfigured lady that I met outside the temple who helped me. If you ever see her, you'd know you have met God as well.

I am so sorry, darling. I am not nearly as strong as you. I tried... I really did. I tried a lot and I tried hard but snapping back to reality is just too painful.

Please take care of my parents and tell them that I am sorry, and I love them a lot. And tell your parents that I love them too, especially your mom, tell her that I love her just a little more. I have wronged you all in so many ways, including this, but I have come to this realisation that there isn't a single moment in my life that I want to live away from my son. It is physically impossible for me, and I don't know how.

So, don't let my loss be in 5 stages for you, instead celebrate my life, celebrate our life. I am just not ready to accept that he was gone, so I want to be with him.

Promise me, that you will remember me with a smile. Promise me that you will cherish every moment of joy in your life. And promise me, that you will let me go.

And one more thing, Punit, I sincerely hope that no mother should ever see her child die.

Until later.

Love you always,
Sanju.'

As Punit read the letter in physical aches, a cold wisp travelled through the room to the outside of the house. The house that held a deep sorrow within, the house that cried for her family.

Sanjana stood outside the gate facing the house and waved a final goodbye. As she turned around, the old disfigured lady and her five-year-old Manu looked at her with tearful eyes. Manu got down from the old lady's lap and held his mother's cold finger.

The old lady slowly walked to the middle of the road and kissed Sanjana's forehead holding her other hand.

All three of them walked on that road into the night that exploded with stars. Sanjana looked at Manu, and she was finally happy.

As the endless sky shone brighter, filling the dark night, it also revealed its biggest secret that most of its brightest lights hold the darkest stories within them.

Connect with the Author

An IITian, Ajinkya is an HR manager by day and a writer by night. He lives in Mumbai and writes psychological thrillers and horrors by city lights. His first book, When The Devil Whispers, a crime thriller based on a real incident is soon going to be turned into a web series.

Instagram: www.instagram.com/bhasmewords/
Facebook: www.facebook.com/bhasmeajinkya/
LinkedIn: www.linkedin.com/in/ajinkya-bhasme/
Twitter: twitter.com/jinky22jan
Website: www.ajinkyabhasme.com

CPSIA information can be obtained
at www.ICGtesting.com
Printed in the USA
LVHW100044280323
742726LV00005B/227

9 789387 131361